Trusting a Tiger

Alaskan Tigers: Book Five

Marissa Dobson

Published by Sunshine Press

Printed in the United States of America

ISBN-13: 978-1-939978-36-3

Dedication

To Thomas—my wonderful husband who's been supportive through everything. He's put up with my late night writing sessions, cooked dinner, over all he's been wonderful. Thank you Thomas.

To my readers who love the Alaskan Tigers as much as I enjoy writing them. Enjoy this newest adventure to Alaska.

Trusting a Tiger: Alaskan Tigers

Acknowledgements

Thank you Jim and Ryan, for the in depth weapons training, for taking the time to go over the differences of each gun, and how to operate them safely. Any mistakes in this book are mine and mine alone.

Trusting a Tiger: Alaskan Tigers

Felix Grady's world came crashing down around him when he received confirmation his twin brother was torturing women. One of the victims was none other than his destined mate. Torn between his twin and protecting his mate and clan, Felix must make the ultimate choice between the two.

Harmony Kirk suffered for years under her former Alpha and Henry. Now in Alaska under the protection of the Alaskan Tigers, she's expected to forget everything that happened and commit herself to the clan. Destined to be the mate of one of the top members of the clan doesn't make things any easier. It doesn't help that the destined mate is the identical twin to the man who spent years abusing her.

Will eliminating Henry make things easier or harder for Harmony? Can she move past Felix's face and see him as a different man than the one who abused her for years? Will it free her from the past she's locked herself into, allowing her to be with the man who is her destiny?

Trusting a Tiger: Alaskan Tigers

Contents

Trusting a Tiger: Alaskan Tigers

Chapter One

The sun glared down from high above when Felix Grady finally stepped out of his cabin. The day off was just what he needed. The long hours he put in while his partner Adam was off mating had worn him out. He slept late and had a leisurely lunch, but now he was tired of doing nothing. He was a tiger that enjoyed being on the move, not lounging around like a bag of lazy bones.

Taking a stroll around the compound would clear his mind before checking in with Ty and Tabitha. He knew Tabitha was in good hands with Adam, but his duties were so engrained in him that he couldn't stop, even for a few hours. It just wasn't the person he was.

Making a circle around the grounds, he checked to be sure all the guards were at their posts, nothing out of the norm. As a last-second change of plan, he turned, deciding to take a detour around the creek. Everyone seemed to love the little area by the creek. There was a little bank where shifters could relax, especially Kallie's mates Taber and Thorben who were able to fish in their bear form without anyone spotting them.

He loved the compound, and the cold weather of Alaska didn't bother him, although he didn't have nearly enough time to enjoy it. Being the Captain of Tabitha's guards takes priority, and with the constant threats to the clans, he rarely had any downtime to enjoy the compound as the other shifters did.

Raja stepped out from around a cabin. "I thought you were taking a day to relax? Checking the grounds at your normal time doesn't break from your routine. You should catch up on much deserved sleep."

Since Raja found his mate, Bethany, he had been more jubilant and full of life. The meaning of life had come back to him in full force. It was a remarkable change from the strict man that he'd been before. Now he lived for more than just his job, he had a mate that he loved. Even his sister Tora had remarked on the change.

"Can't keep me out of the action for long." He chuckled. "My tiger was restless and demanded I get back to some resemblance of my routine. Any updates?"

"Not yet. Connor and Lukas are working on finding Henry and Randolph, but no solid leads. Recently they found out Randolph spent years being Pierce's second, but he's awfully quiet so far for the death of his leader. Speaking of it, have you seen Harmony on your walk? I stopped by her studio, and she wasn't there." Raja came to stand next to Felix looking out over the creek bubbling its way down the path.

"No. I heard the guards have been taken off her door after she complained. Is that the wisest move?" There was something about

Harmony that drove him to her. She was so scared and frightened, yet he could sense something hiding under the surface, drawing him to her. Maybe it was the person she used to be before his twin brother ruined the shine she had.

"You heard the stink she put up—did you want to listen to that long-term?" Raja shook his head. "Plus, we don't know when Henry might actually make his move, and we can't keep her under lock and key indefinitely. Robin will feel if she's in any danger, and we're counting on warning from you before he arrives."

"I'll do what I can." Being Henry's twin should have made it easier for him to determine Henry's next move, but he was almost as blind to it as everyone else. Harmony might be their only early warning when it came to Henry's final move.

Raja patted Felix on the back. "I better get back to Bethany. It's our night for the family dinner. Enjoy the rest of your night off."

Felix nodded, with a slight envy eating at him. His Lieutenant had a family that most of the clan was envious of. Most tiger shifter off-springs ended up leaving their home clan when they grew up to search for another one to make their name in, separating families across the country. Most shifters don't have a loyalty to a family like humans do. The loyalty was only to their mate and clan. Parents and siblings were a different category altogether for shifters. Siblings normally remained close though the distances, but parents seemed to have more distances. It's believed to come from their beast since that was how they were in the wild.

Raja and Tora had been close all their lives, and Tora mating did little to separate the siblings. What separation might have happened was closed with the birth of Tora and Marcus' daughter Scarlet. Since mating with Bethany, the family dinners have been rotated between Tora's cabin and Raja's, giving each woman a chance to host.

With family and mating on his mind, he decided to extend his walk down the creek bed before going back to check on Tabitha. The lush trees lined the creek, keeping it hidden even from the cabins. It was a safe and secure spot deep within the compound, one you were never sure who you would find there.

A familiar scent of honeysuckle and toasted vanilla teased him further along the path to one of the hiding spaces that Kallie favored when she first came to the clan. There, hidden amongst the trees, Harmony sat with her back pressed against the base of one of the trees, tossing rocks at the creek.

"Harmony." He called to her before stepping closer because he didn't want to scare her. He knew that just the sight of him made her tense, serving as a reminder of the man that forced himself on her. It was still hard for him to believe that his twin had done such an unimaginable thing. They were raised better than that, and having the tiger inside him but being unable to shift was not enough of an excuse for Felix to forgive Henry's behavior.

She slid her legs up tight against her chest and met his gaze, but she didn't speak. She watched him like a tiger stalking its prey, but she wasn't strong enough to take him down. In tiger form, he outweighed her by more than a hundred pounds, but even as a human, she was no match for him. His years of training and hours in the gym meant he could take her down without hurting her and without much effort at all.

"You okay?" He stepped closer, keeping in her line of sight and his hand way from the gun in his shoulder holster.

"I can't take it any longer." She leaned her head against the tree and looked at him. "I can't stand the fear, the panic. Damn it, to be a prisoner, it's like being with him all over again. I keep waiting for him to find me, to make me pay for running."

"You're safe here. He's not going to get to you. I won't let him. Do you understand that?" He knelt in front of her, just far enough away that they didn't touch, still respecting her space.

"You can't be sure of that. There are so many threats against your clan now, with the Texas clan and the rogues." Her jaw was set as she stared at him. He could read it in her body language that she didn't believe him.

"I told you I'll protect you, and I will. There are always threats to clans, but that doesn't change my vow to protect you." He paused, listening to the quietness, when an idea struck him. "I know you're feeling boxed in, so how about if we take a drive? There's no need to go into town or anything, but a drive through the area might help you recharge and get outside of the compound for a bit. What do you say?"

"I don't know."

He could feel her hesitation. "If we're going to live together in the same clan, you'll need to move past your apprehension of me. I understand why you have it, but I can't change my looks or what Henry did to you. I also know words don't mean much, but I'm nothing like he is. Let me prove it. There's somewhere I want to show you." He stood. "What do you say?"

She nodded. "Okay. To get out of here, even just for a short time, would be heavenly."

He smiled at her. "I need to swing by to see Tabitha and get the keys for one of the guards' SUVs then we can go. Ten minutes."

She stood and brushed off the butt of her jeans. "Should I meet you somewhere then or something?"

"Come along—it's fine. I'm off-duty today, but I want to check in with Adam." He led the way up the creek a bit further until they came to a small footbridge to cross back over. There were so many things he wanted to ask her, but he didn't. Spooking her would only send her back into her retreat, and it took too long to get her out of her tigress form to risk anything that might send her back. He'd wait until she was ready.

Silence fell over them like a warm blanket. The only thing heard was the crunch of the occasional stick under his boots. There were no birds that frequented the area—too many tigers and bears in the area that scared them off. Felix always enjoyed the quiet, but now in the quiet he found his thoughts full of the woman standing next to him.

"Hey, Felix," Tabitha called to him as they stepped out of the trees.

"Tabitha and Adam, just the people I was on my way to see. What are you doing out here?" Felix quickly scanned the grounds, checking for any threat.

"Robin's down with a cold and asked me to check on Harmony," Adam explained.

"I do hope Robin is all right." The common cold was not something Felix or the other shifters had to deal with, only their human counterparts. Once a shifter went through the change, they couldn't catch a cold or the flu, which came in quite handy. Even though Robin was human, she would gain a higher tolerance to illness from her mating, making illness uncommon. The Alpha/clan bond between Robin and Harmony was highly unusual, especially considering Robin was human, but it was there. Robin had no idea how to handle the connection as a shifter automatically did, so it was becoming a learning process for her. In the meantime, the connection was draining her to the point of illness.

"Bethany healed her, so she should be back to normal soon." Tabitha nodded.

Felix accompanied Robin on her daily visits with Harmony a few times a week, trying to get her used to his presence. Robin was working closely with Harmony to get her to open up and to work past what Henry put her through.

"I was going to take Harmony out for a drive. She's suffering with a little cabin fever, and I thought a little time off the grounds would give us both a break." He almost asked if they would like to join, but instead he kept it to himself. It wasn't for Harmony's sake but because he wanted to be with her without the others gathered around. He felt the need to prove to her that he was nothing like Henry.

Harmony wasn't the first woman to see him as a threat or to fear him, and in most cases, that's what he needed. With Tabitha's security on the line, he had to seem like a bastard that would do what he threatened. His threat should come from his actions and body language not necessarily from words. However, when it came to Harmony, he was going out of his way to see that she didn't fear him. *Why?*

* * *

Trees whipped past the SUV window as Harmony and Felix headed further and further away from the compound. Her heart beat frantically against her ribs, her mind racing through her fears. She could taste her pulse in her throat. What if this was a trap? He could be leading her to Henry. After all, they were twins—surely they had some bond.

"You're going to have Robin calling." Felix never turned his gaze away from the road.

"What?"

"Your fear. If I can feel it this strongly, I wouldn't be surprised if Robin calls and orders me to return you to the compound at once." He looked over at her. "Maybe this wasn't such a good idea. Do you want me to take you back?"

Part of her wanted to scream 'yes,' but if he were taking her to Henry would he have offered to take her back to the compound? She didn't think so. More importantly, Robin trusted Felix, therefore she was trying to. He might look like the man who had raped and tortured her for months, leaving scars all over her body, but from what she saw of him, he was different.

Staying in Alaska close to Robin, the only person she had any loyalties to, she'd have to trust Felix and the other clan members. This was the first step on the long road to the life she once had. Not that she ever thought she'd be the person she once was. "No, I want to go."

"I know you're scared. I should have asked someone else to come, but with Robin a little under the weather, I was out of people you trusted. We could do this another day when Robin can come with us."

Pawing at her jeans, she tried to wipe the sweat that had coated her palms away. "It's fine. I wanted to get out. You know Adam wouldn't have wanted Robin to leave the security of the compound without him, and you both couldn't have left Tabitha unguarded."

"Then Adam could take you and Robin, and I will stay at the compound."

"No." She turned away from the window to look at him. "Felix, I want to trust you, and I'm trying."

"I understand. Every time you look at me, it's hard for you to see me as someone other than Henry. It's going to be over soon."

Hadn't she heard that since she arrived at the compound? It had been weeks of sitting around waiting for Henry to either attack or for someone to find him. In all that time, her leg nearly healed from the nasty bear trap wound. She was tired of waiting—if only she could do something about it. Even if Henry couldn't shift, he had proven more than once she was no match for him.

"There's a slight difference in your features. Your jawbone is a little more rounded, the dimples are a little deeper, and your eyes are different. They still hold the edge of danger, but there's a touch of understand and friendliness to them. The biggest difference between you two is your attitude. He's, well…"

"Insane?" he supplied.

"Yes." She shrugged. It was awful to say it aloud, but it was the truth. "I'm sorry."

"There's no need to apologize. It's true, and I've known it for years. When we turned eighteen, our parents moved to Australia so they didn't have to deal with it any longer. The tiger inside him has driven him crazy from not being able to shift. The only difference between Henry and a rogue is that rogues are put down when the tiger takes over. Looks like Henry's fate will be finding him at last." Felix turned the SUV onto a dirt road, doing his best to avoid the potholes.

She felt her eyes narrow down at him, watching him intently. "Even though he's your brother, you'll kill him?"

He slid the SUV into Park and looked at her. "Yes. Brother or not, he can't do what he's done and get away with it. There's no other recourse for what he's done." He let out a deep sigh. "Years ago, when the tiger first started to drive him toward madness, I wanted to do it then, before he could cause any problems. It might seem heartless to some, but we're not like humans. There's not a hospital we can put him in. It's what our kind does when one is sick, we put them out of their misery. Henry is driven by his madness. He's no longer the brother I grew up with."

Without thinking, she reached across the gap and laid her hand on his lap. It's what their kind did when someone hurt. Touch gave them comfort. Her fingers brushed against the back of his hand, and unexpected electricity shot through her. "*No!*" Tears welled in her eyes with the knowledge of what that meant. *Oh, shit—it can't be!*

Trusting a Tiger: Alaskan Tigers

Chapter Two

Electricity coursed through Felix, stealing his breath and all intelligent thought. Could this truly be happening? How could fate mate him with the woman his twin tortured? He would constantly serve as a reminder of her past—a reminder of the hell that she went through to regain her freedom.

How did he not see this week's ago when Bethany healed Harmony's leg? After all, he held her down—his hands were clasped around her ankles…no skin-to-skin contact. Damn, that's how he missed it. For the mating to start, it had to be triggered from skin contact.

He opened the SUV's door, putting one foot on the running board. "Come on." He stepped out, shut the door and moved to the front of SUV, leaving her to join him or stay in the car. At that moment, he wasn't sure what he'd prefer her to do…all he knew was that he couldn't believe his luck. It ate at him that the mate he knew he'd find one day was so distraught by his features. If it was something he could change, he would have, but this was beyond his scope of modification.

Now he knew why he was drawn to her, it was because she was his mate. Even without touching her, his tiger was able to sense it in her. His tiger's eagerness toward her and the way he was drawn to her like a bug to a light should have warned him.

He should have known and ran for the hills. To leave the clan at least for a time, away from Harmony would have been better for her then being mated with him. They could have been brought together in another time and place and maybe things would have worked for them. Here and now, what hope did they have for a happy mating? They'd be forced together, neither of them able to deny the mating once the painful desire kicked in.

He looked out over the valley, the trees full of green and life again after a long winters rest. From the hillside he realized just how small he was in the whole scheme of things. Even after years in Alaska, he never got used to the beauty of the land, there was always something to cherish. This was his home, the land he'd fight for, just as he would for his clan.

Harmony came to stand next to him. "You can't just pretend that didn't happen. It's not just going to go away."

"I know that, but, damn it, what am I supposed to do? This isn't the mating I expected. We both know I can't just push you up against the side of the SUV and claim you as mine."

"What are we going to do?" She leaned against the bumper.

That was the million-dollar question. Did he have any hope of winning over the woman his brother served to alienate? "What do you want to do about it?" He turned enough toward her to watch the emotions play over her face. It was a rainbow of emotions from anger to disappointment, finally settling on sadness. He could see it glistening in her eyes, but still she remained silent, having no more answers then he did.

Just watching her, her long ruby-red hair flying around her face from the wind, he wanted to pull her against his body, run his hand through her hair until she was close enough to press his lips to hers. "There's no reason to deny it. I can see your anger and sadness over this mating, but I don't know how to change this. When Taber and Thorben first mated with Kallie, they looked to see if there was a way out of it—there isn't. So it doesn't leave us with many options."

"I won't deny it, you're not my first choice for a mate. Damn it, if I'm to have a mate now while there's this threat of Henry looming, I want a mate that I can cuddle next to at night and know I'm protected. Not fear every bump and noise of the night."

He spun around on her, his body inches from the front of her forcing her back against the SUV. "Don't stand there and imply that I've done anything but protect you since you've arrive at the clan. Robin and I have done everything we could to make you feel safe here. To imply otherwise does a huge disservice to not only me but to Robin. She's been dividing her time between Adam and you and has been driving herself to exhaustion."

"I didn't mean…"

"If Robin isn't there with you, she's working with Connor going over leads trying to find something that hints to where Henry is. That woman is doing more for you than is expected, after all she's human.

She's mated to a shifter, but that doesn't change that she still needs sleep, food, and can still occasionally become ill. She has put her own needs aside so she could see that Henry was no longer a threat to you." He laid a hand on either side of her on the SUV. "She's even the one that's stays on top of the Elders to make sure that Henry is dealt with before they go deal with the Texas clan. She's risking a lot for you and how do you repay her? By standing here implying you're alone with no one to protect you."

"Damn it, if you'd let me finish."

"Go ahead." He took his hands from the hood and stepped back.

"I didn't mean to imply that. I only meant…" She threw her hand up in the air. "Oh never mind, you wouldn't understand."

"You're right I don't, not completely, but try me. What can it hurt?"

"I've always been reserved, never the go-getter of the clan. I realize and accept I'm a weaker shifter then a lot of the clan members, but I don't go looking for fights. Even living with the Ohio clan, I spent most of my time alone. I don't understand clan living and being surrounded by people. To have one person that I can rely on, his loyalty to me above all, and who can help me though this world would be a blessing." She stepped away from the SUV moving forward to look out over the hillside. "Robin has her mate and the clan. Not to mention Tex that she's helping with his abuse under the Texas Alpha. As you said, I'm making her sick because I need her too much. I'm just tired of being alone. You—well you have

Tabitha and your duties. Other than that, who do I have? I'm alone and downright scared."

He stepped up behind her, laying his hand on her shoulder to guide her around to look at him. "We can't do anything about this mating—nor can I change my face or who I am—but I can be what you need. Harmony, I've been protecting you since you've came to the clan, that's not going to change. On the same hand neither will my duties to the clan. I've worked too hard to be where I am to give it all up, and I wouldn't want to be just a clan member again. I can't go from being in the action to living the life of a member again. Given a chance, we could find a balance and work through it."

"I don't know if I can or how it will ever work."

"That you'll need to think about. In the meantime, how about I help you with protection? You might not be able to stand up to stronger shifters physically, but there's always an equalizer." He put his hand on the butt of the gun sticking from his shoulder holster. "A gun will make the playing fields more equal for you and give you a chance to get away."

"I've never shot a gun before. I don't know if I could kill someone."

"Anyone will tell you that you should never point a gun at anyone that you're not willing to kill, but when it comes to shifters, only a shot through the heart or in the head will kill us. A gun will give you a chance to get away." He ran his finger across her shoulder. "Don't get me wrong—I believe you're safe on the compound, but it could give you a piece of mind. I will teach you how to shoot if you're interested."

"I'll learn, but I don't know if I can shoot someone." Even through the reservation in her voice there was a hint of excitement about learning to protect herself.

"Learning is the first step. We'll conquer your reservations next." He pulled the gun from his holster. Using his thumb, he ejected the magazine and shoved it in his pocket. "When you take ahold of the gun, it's your gun and no one should be able to take it away from you. You hold it tight, but not tight enough that you can break the handle or that your muscles strain under the pressure."

He pulled back the top of the gun showing her it was empty. "There's no bullets in it now with the magazine out. You have no chance of shooting anything. I want you to hold it just like I was, just to get a feel of it."

"Okay." She took the gun from his hand, doing her best to copy his moves. Holding it out before her like it might bite her.

"Now with your right hand, cup the grip with your palm, making sure there's no air pockets." He nodded, watching as she did it. "Pretty good. I'm just going to adjust your hands. Think of it as loaded and remember to keep your fingers off the trigger until you're ready to shoot." He curled his hand around her left one, forcing her fingers around the gun to lie on top of the right hand fingers. "Keep your hands together because they will give you stability.

"Now lay that thumb on top of the other. This gun doesn't have an external safety. It has an extra-long trigger that acts as your safety.

On guns with a safety, your top right thumb will be used to take off the safety. Just holding it, how does it feel?" He removed his hands from hers, but still stayed close, his chest brushing against her arm.

"Dangerous." She let a nervous laugh.

"Good, you never want to forget that. Even shooting a shifter somewhere they can heal, it will serve to piss them off, so you need to get away before they can heal it. But it will give you a way to protect yourself. To have it in the back of your mind that you can protect yourself if anything happens, does that not outweigh your fears of the gun?"

"Somewhat."

"Very well. Wait here." He stepped back from her, walking the couple steps back to the SUV.

"What are you doing?" She turned to him, holding the gun at the ground.

"Getting you a target, we'll do some target practice up here." He pulled out a sheet of paper with a large red bull's eye from the back, along with a box of bullets.

"Here?" She asked looking around at the area.

"It's private property, why not?" He walked past her to the post just before the trees and stapled the target to it.

"Private property? Are we trespassing?" Fear creeping back into her voice.

He came to stand beside her, taking the gun from her and sliding the magazine back into it. "No, the clan owns it. Look below us…that's the compound. All I did was bring you around the back of it where the steep mountainside behind the creek is. If we could jump down and live, you'd find yourself almost in the same spot I found you by the creek."

He held the gun in his hand to keep him from wrapping his arm around her waist. "This is one of my favorite stops when I get some down time. It's beautiful to stand here and see the home I've worked so hard to protect. Now come on, let's see how you do."

He could feel her pulse speed. "I don't know."

"Nerves are good, but just try it once." He held the gun out to her. "It's loaded, so remember to keep your finger off the trigger until you're ready to shoot. All I want you to do is take it into your hands again. Once you have the position again, we'll go from there."

She took the gun from him, careful to avoid the trigger area. Wrapping her hands around it, she took a deep breath. "Is this right?"

"Almost." He adjusted her hand, moving her fingers slightly. "Remember, no air pockets around the handle."

She turned enough to look at him but kept the gun pointed straight ahead at the target. "What if I shoot someone and get brought up on murder charges?"

"That's not going to happen. You're not going to kill someone that isn't trying to harm you. If you do it with witnesses that aren't shifters, they'll see you were defending yourself and no charges will be brought against you. Alaska has a Stand Your Ground law, but none of this matters. We deal with those issues, the bodies and everything. The important thing is to protect yourself." He slid his hand around her waist.

"But what if…"

"Harmony, you're worrying for nothing. You won't do it to someone who isn't trying to kill you. Right now, all I want you to do is shoot it here for target practice. There's no way you're going to hurt anyone right now. If you decide you're willing to keep a gun on you, we'll face that next." When she continued to stare at him, he added. "My view has always been 'it's better to be judged by twelve than carried by six,' but it will have to be your choice. Just try shooting the gun, and we'll deal with all the other stuff later."

She nodded, turning back to the target and positioning her hands as they were before. "Let's do this."

Her nerves teased along the edges of his skin, creating goosebumps. The point of teaching her to shoot and carry a gun was for her protection and to make her feel more ease, but it would only work if she was comfortable with the gun. He wouldn't force her to carry a weapon that she wasn't comfortable with. It would only increase the chances of it being used against her. "Okay, look down the length of the gun. Those three dots you see are your sights. You'll look down between these two and aim the one single dot over where you want the bullet to go. In this case, you'll aim it so it's over the bull's eye. Look between the first two dots, not over them, and down at the last to the target. There should be equal amount of light on each side of your third sight."

"Okay, I have it centered over the target, now what?" Her arms shook slightly with nerves.

"Take a deep breath and gently squeeze the trigger when you're ready." He stood next to her, careful not to touch her so not to spoil her concentration.

The bang of the bullet exiting the chamber cut through the silence, filling the air with the smell of gunpowder, and Harmony let out a surprised squeal. "It's okay, you're fine."

She lowered the weapon toward the ground. "I'm sorry. I didn't expect that."

Caressing the small of her back, he nodded. "The first time it can be scary, but look—you shot just to the right of the bullseye. That's amazing for your first shot. See if you can do it again."

With each shot, she became more at ease with the weapon in her hand and liberated. He watched as her nerves and fears over the gun were replaced by the liberation of being about to protect herself. She'd no longer have to feel being at someone's mercy again, and that made him feel good. This was one step to overcoming the wall that Henry erected between them.

Chapter Three

Harmony lounged on the bed, glaring at the gun that sat on the bedside table. Somehow she let Felix talk her into taking a gun back to her room. Target practice went better than she could have expected. She was actually a pretty good shot for never holding a gun before and most of her nerves died away with practice. Yet there was still something tingling inside her that made her hesitate, a gun was nothing to mess with. Felix assured her that with more practice she'd be completely comfortable with the gun and had promised to take her out shooting as often as she wanted.

A knock at her door pulled her thoughts away from the gun and Felix. Rolling over onto her back, she sniffed the air to find out who was at her door without getting up. "Come in."

Robin entered, her thin frame looking even slimmer than normal, and the light circles under her eyes screamed to anyone looking that Robin wasn't sleeping enough. Felix's words rang in Harmony's mind again. Robin was doing too much. She needed to focus on her mate not on Harmony's problems. Her blue jeans and short-sleeved blouse looked comfortable and ready for anything, but the heels are what caught Harmony's attention. It had been months since she'd worn heels, she missed the way her legs looked in them. Maybe she could order a few things online to spice up her wardrobe.

"Sorry I didn't get to come by yesterday, I was feeling ill. I heard Felix took you out for a drive." Robin strolled closer to the bed.

"Yesterday was an eye-opening day. I wanted to talk to you about something." She moved her legs so that Robin could sit on the bed. "Felix told me you're spending extra time with Connor going through everything that they find. You're doing too much, and you're making yourself sick and for what? We'll eventually find Henry."

"You sound too much like Adam for my tastes today." Robin dragged her hand through her curly long brown hair. "That's a big change from two days ago. You were dying for someone to find him—you even threatened to go out and start looking for him yourself. What brought this on?"

"Yesterday with Felix, being outside of the compound, it's just what I needed. I've been here weeks now, and it's time I start living again." She moved close enough so she could lay her hand over Robin's. "Henry is not only a threat to me and this clan but to everyone. I'm not saying that we should give up the search, but I want you to back off a little. You're freshly mated. You should be enjoying your mate not wrapped up in my issues."

"How can I be otherwise when I feel your pain when you speak of him?" Robin pushed off the bed, closing the small space between the bed and window she gazed outside. "I've seen what he did to you, how can I not do something?"

"You've what?" Anger, sadness, and a mixture of other emotions raced through Harmony. She never wanted anyone to know the shit she went through with Henry. They were her dark secrets, to know someone else knew it was embarrassing.

"These visions come to me in dreams, yet I know without a doubt they are real. They're your memories." Robin turned back to Harmony, sadness in her eyes. "I've only spoken to Adam about it. I couldn't keep it from my mate, he knew something was wrong when I woke in a cold sweat. It's hard to hide anything from your mate when they can feel your emotions. He believes this connection between us is giving me your dreams, and he wanted to talk to Ty about it to be certain. Ty being Alpha of the clan and having the same connection to his people that I share with you might give us some insight on this. He might know of a way for me to block them."

"You're having my dreams. You see it all don't you? Everything Henry did to me?"

Robin nodded. "I'm afraid so."

"Felix is taking me to speak with Ty and Tabitha this afternoon, so I'll bring up the subject. If he can help, I'm sure he'll meet with you afterwards. Maybe committing myself to the Alaskan Tigers could relieve the strain of my emotions on you." She scooted up on the bed, pressing her back against the headboard and running her hand along the red and black satin comforter. Oh, how she loved the bed and comforter. It was so much more than she'd had in more years than she cared to remember, but the colors, she knew, made her seem paler than she was.

"You're thinking about committing to the clan?" Robin turned to face her.

"I might have no choice. If I'm to be mated with Felix, I'll have to." Things were so confusing when it came to her mating. When Felix wasn't there, her body and tigress longed for him, but when he was there, she would do almost anything to get away from him. Sharing the face with the man who raped her for sport countless times was almost more than she could bear, not to mention the torture he put her thought just to hear her scream.

"Felix?" Robin's eyes grew as big as saucers with both amusement and concern.

"Yeah, I know. It's a really screwed-up situation, but what are we to do?"

"I thought there was something different about you when I walked in, but I wasn't sure what. Maybe we should talk about this, I'm sure this is bringing up more memories of what you went through." Robin came away from the window, her gaze fully on Harmony as she sat back down on the edge of the bed.

"It hasn't brought up anything I wasn't already dealing with. Either way, right now I don't need a therapist; I need a friend." Harmony wasn't sure Robin could be anything than what she had been, but she didn't want to be analyzed now. She wanted someone to tell her that things would work out. After all, they had to…didn't they?

"I'm that, too. I'm just concerned about the progress we made. I don't want this to set you back. I'm not sure I completely understand this mating thing. I can feel it between Adam and I, but I don't really understand how it works. Do you have the right to deny your mate?"

"Not really. Eventually the desire between the mates will be so overwhelming and painful that it will force the two together. A human mate wouldn't feel it as strongly as shifters do because our desire would keep our beast on edge until we gave in." She tugged her sweater down, straightening all the winkles from it. "I know Felix is a different person, but…" She let the words die on her tongue.

"But he looks identical to Henry," Robin supplied.

"Yes. Every time he's around, it's impossible for me to deny what happened in Ohio. Felix brings it all back to the forefront of my mind. There are slight differences in their features if you look closely but they are still identical twins. Personality-wise, they are completely different, and there's no mistaking one for the other."

"The biggest question is: can you get over what he reminds you of, or will that always be a sore spot in the mating?" Robin nodded to the gun on the nightstand. "What's that all about?"

"Felix took me target practicing yesterday." She couldn't help but smile as warmth filled her with the memories of the afternoon they spent together. "He gave me a way to protect myself, to 'liberate me from my fears,' as he would say."

"Protection isn't a bad thing if you're comfortable with it. When I was on the run from Pierce and his rogues, I had a handgun. When Adam found me holed up in a crumby motel room and brought me back here, he let me keep it, knowing it would give me comfort since I was terrified of him—of everything even my own bloody shadow. It gave me peace of mind knowing that with it I stood a chance of getting away from a shifter. Are you comfortable with it?"

She nodded. "Getting there. We spent a good part of yesterday shooting it until I got comfortable. He's bringing me a hip holster when he comes back, and we'll go to the range on the compound after I speak with Ty."

"Seems as though you two are getting along well. I told you he's a good man. He'll be a good mate if you can overcome your past. Maybe when Henry is no longer a threat, it will be easier." Robin ran her hand over the comforter smoothing out the wrinkles. "You know, if you need anything, I'm here for you, or if you want to talk, I'm always here for you."

She nodded, knowing Robin was eager to get back to her mate. "I know, thank you. But I'm serious—I do want you to take a break from helping Connor. I have a feeling everything's going to work out."

"Okay." That single word didn't seem very convincing, but it's all Robin gave. "All right, I promised Adam I wouldn't be long, so I better get going before he's knocking down your door." Robin rose from the bed, plastering a smile on her face.

"Go enjoy your mate." Harmony wondered if there would ever be a time when she could do the same. Accepting Felix as her mate might be the hardest task before her.

Robin moved through the small studio apartment, making her way to the door before she turned back. "Oh, I forgot, Kallie invited us to have lunch at her place tomorrow with Bethany and Tabitha. Are you interested in going?"

"Sure." It was time she started getting out of her hidey-hole, but if she were honest with herself, she'd have to admit it wasn't just getting out. It was also the fact that with Tabitha there she'd at least get another glimpse of Felix. Damn her mixed feelings about him— damn everything that happened that led her here.

"Wonderful, I'll be over just before noon tomorrow, and we'll go together. Call me if you need me." Robin closed the door behind her, leaving Harmony alone again.

For years she had spent her time alone, enjoying the peace of it, but now the silence was deafening. Though she was a member of the Ohio clan most of her life, she was never a part of the clan. She had a place in the woods away from everyone and everything, never bothering with clan life until her Alpha called her. The life suited her until that final challenge from her Alpha—the one she failed, landing her in Henry's hands.

She tried to push the thoughts of Henry away, to enjoy the silence, turning her thoughts to Felix. But no longer was silence enjoyable—Henry had seen to that. There was no longer anything easy about life. She didn't want to be alone, but she couldn't stand to be surrounded by people, either.

She focused her thoughts on Felix, trying to change away the anxiety that thinking about Henry raised. Could she find a way to

Trusting a Tiger: Alaskan Tigers

look past the looks that reminded her of the horror she went through and cherish the man she was destined to be with?

The cell phone she picked up on her run rang, sending panic through her. In all her time at the compound, not once had the phone rang. She only purchased it after she escaped Henry's confinement in case of emergencies. No one had that number. Figuring it was a wrong number, she debated not answering.

Timidly she grabbed the phone, bringing it to her ear. "Hello?"

"You thought you could run to my brother for protection, and I wouldn't find you?" Henry's angry voice filled the line, stealing her breath. "I'm coming for you. It won't be long now."

"How did you get this number?" Her hand shook so much she was surprised she was able to keep the phone pressed to her ear.

"Stupid bitch," he spat, "you registered the phone in your own name when you got the number. After that, it wasn't hard to find you. Randolph knows what he's doing. I paid him well to find it, and for that you'll be screaming for forgiveness when I get my hands on you."

"I just want you to leave me alone!"

His voice sounded angrier. "Do you know why I chose to keep you alive when all the other ones they sent me died within hours from the torture?" When she didn't say anything, he continued. "I knew you were to be mated with Felix. I could sense it. He won't have you when I'll have no mate. If you thought the sex was painful before, it will be tenfold now that you've found your mate." With that the line went dead, leaving her in more of a panic then she already was.

She knew he was coming for her, but now she couldn't help wondering how he knew she was in Alaska. Felix's connection to Henry was strained and didn't work like it would if both twins could shift, but how did Henry's connection to Felix work? Was it strong, more accurate? Or was it as simple as tracing the phone?

Trusting a Tiger: Alaskan Tigers

Chapter Four

Felix nearly ran to Harmony's studio, his tiger on edge all day with eagerness to be with his mate. There was a tingling sensation that something wasn't right, but he couldn't figure out what it was. Without the mating being complete he couldn't feel her emotions completely. He knew without a doubt that she was still on the compound grounds and was in no immediate danger.

For some mates, it was easy for them to feel each other's feelings before the mating had been complete, but since she had no connection to his clan, it was adding to the strain. He was only left with bits and pieces of her emotions. When the mate was a human, it allowed things to be free flowing, and the shifter would feel everything from the moment the mate was found.

Jogging across the compound, he took a moment to enjoy the crisp summer air. Summer in this part of Alaska rarely got above sixty degrees and always reminded him more of fall in the lower forty-eight. Either way, he enjoyed living here with the coolness and picturesque surroundings. He could never picture himself leaving Alaska—it was his home now.

A cool breeze slid through him—Henry was on the move. There was a tingle of happiness in Henry...and eagerness. Was it eagerness to find Harmony? Felix still wasn't sure where Henry was. All he could feel was that Henry was nearing them, still not in Alaska but definitely closer than he was before. If he continued to move at the pace he was, he'd be in Alaska within two days. *Shit!*

They needed to locate him before he could get near the compound. He didn't want to put Harmony or any of the other clan at risk. Deciding not to mention it to Harmony now—after all, there was no reason to worry her more when there was still nothing that could be done—he gave a quick knock, and when he received no answer, he pushed her door open. He could sense her but didn't see her immediately, and in a studio apartment the size of a master bedroom in most houses, that sent the alarm bells ringing. "Harmony?"

Shutting the door he stepped around the other side of the bed, planning to check that bathroom before heading down to the creek where he found her yesterday. There she was curled into a ball, her legs pulled tight against her chest and her face buried in the tops of her knees.

He dropped to his knees in front of her. "What is it? What has happened?"

She didn't look up, only sobbed louder. He cursed not being able to feel her emotions completely. He laid his hand on her leg, and when she didn't pull away, he moved closer, wrapping his arm around her shoulders. She fit against his body as if she should have always been there. Warm and snug the other half of him. "Shhh, Harmony. Whatever it is, we'll get through it."

She snuggled her head against his chest, clinging to him. What had happened to cause her such distress? When he bumped into Robin earlier, she mentioned the progress Harmony was making and had even agreed to lunch at Kallie's the next day. That was a huge step forward for Harmony, but this seemed to be a step in the opposite direction. He held her, letting her cry, knowing that when she was ready to tell him what happened, she would. Forcing her would only delay things further.

He wasn't sure how long they sat there with his arm around her, until she finally looked up at him. Her eyes were bloodshot and her face was tearstained, making him angry that someone or something had upset his mate.

"Henry called." Her voice was raw from crying.

"What? How?" His angry level rose like a thermometer on a blistering hot day.

"He found the number of the cell phone I purchased when I ran from Ohio."

He ran his hand down the length of her arm. "What did he say?"

Shaking her head, the tears began to flow again.

"I need to know what he said. Something in it might give us a clue to where he is." As much as she might not want to think about it, he had to know. It could mean finding Henry before he arrived at the compound.

"He said nothing about his location, but he knows I'm here. He believes I knew you were his brother before I arrived and sought you out for your help." She stretched her legs out before her, her body still pressed against his.

"There had to be something else to make you this upset. Harmony, I need to know."

"He knew I was to be your mate. It's why all this happened, and that's why he's coming after me." She wriggled free from his embrace and stood. "He said that you've had everything in life while he's been left on the sidelines, and he won't let you have your mate—that I'm to be his."

He stood and reached out to her. "I'm not going to let him get to you again. I'll protect you."

How Henry find out she was to be his mate, he didn't know, but other things became clearer. Henry forced himself on Harmony with the hope that he could take over the mating, stealing his mate. Even though twins shared the same DNA, it didn't work like that for tigers. Twin bear shifters could mate with the same person as Taber and Thorben did with Kallie, but it didn't work the same way with tigers. Tiger shifters would never share a mate because they were too possessive.

Sex with someone other than your mate was uncomfortable before the mating commenced, even painful for some, but would be excruciating after the mating was started. If Henry got his hands on Harmony now, there was no doubt that she'd wished she were dead from the agonizing pain. He couldn't let her fall back into Henry's paws, no matter the cost.

"How did he know I was here? That I was your mate?" Questions flowed without giving him time to answer.

"If your number is listed, it wouldn't be too hard for someone to find it. I doubt Henry did—his insanity wouldn't have let him—but maybe Randolph. Once he had the number, he could have tracked the phone." He wrapped his arm around her, turning her to face him. "I don't know how he found out we were to be mated. Maybe he could feel a dull connection to you. Maybe there was a Seer who told him. I don't know, but we'll find out."

"Randolph found my number." She shook her head. "I don't care any longer, I just want it to be over."

He pulled her into his body, wrapping his arms around her and hugged her to him. "It will be soon, I promise." She wrapped her arms around his waist, clinging to him.

He'd see Henry dead for causing his mate so much pain and heartache. No longer would he stand by and let their blood bond or sympathy stand in the way of what needed to be done. His parents already resented him for his stance on Henry and most likely it would get worse when he killed Henry, but he wouldn't let that stand in his way either. He never understood his parents, leaving the country to put as much distance as they could between them and Henry while refusing to take action to prevent Henry from hurting others. No longer, Felix would handle the situation if his parents wanted to live in denial. His mate was more important than any blood bond he had.

* * *

With Felix meeting with the Elders, Harmony slid into the blistering hot tub. She needed something to wash away the memories of her past and relax her strained muscles before she had to meet with the Elders as well. The hot water worked the tension away from her, she slid deep into the garden tub, resting her head against the top. The bubbles teased around her neck, sending the sweet lavender scent in each breath, relaxing her from the inside out.

It had only been twenty-four hours since she found out that Felix was her mate, and already her tigress paced within her for his touch. Her beast forced her to begin working through the issues that had been a solid wall between Felix and her. The walls were beginning to crumble away, and the proof of that was in the way she clung to him seeking his comfort. She wanted his arms around her, to feel his caresses. No longer did she turn from him because of what he reminded her of.

She was beginning to see him as his own person and not an extension of Henry. Was she ready for their mating? Not yet, but she was getting there. Good thing since she wasn't sure how much longer her beast would wait before forcing the issue.

Worries still lingered within her. What if Felix and Henry were working together? Sliding under the water and wetting her hair, she realized how absorbed that was. If she really wanted to know, to make sure Felix was on her side, there was one way to guarantee it. *Mating.* After mating, whatever commitment he had to Henry would be gone because of the mating bond. If Felix was working with his brother, he wouldn't be able to betray her to Henry.

Shaking her head, she knew he wasn't working with Henry. Even that tingle of doubt was just her fear working overtime. She'd make sure before she mated with him. After all, she didn't want to be mated to someone who would have betrayed her given half the chance.

Felix's vow to protect her played out in her mind again. He would never bring trouble to his clan. He was committed to them and to her. The bath water was growing cold, but at least it served to help her work through any lingering doubt she had when it came to Felix. He was her mate, he wouldn't risk her, and he was too responsible and caring to work with Henry. He'd have never stood for Henry's behavior if he had known.

Refreshing the water with heat, she knew that her mating would be complete soon, making it more dangerous if Henry got his hands on her but worth the connection to Felix. She wanted her mate in every way that she was meant to have him.

Trusting a Tiger: Alaskan Tigers

Chapter Five

Felix stood in Ty's quarters, updating Ty to the latest on Henry. There had to be something they could do to find him before he arrived. Felix didn't want Henry to get close enough to the compound to cause any trouble.

"I want her cell phone destroyed. You can give her one of the secure ones we have on hand. Can you recognize the location where Henry is at all?" Ty looked up from his laptop.

"Not really. It's deserted, there are mountains in the distance, and it's warm. I think he's somewhere in the West, possibly Wyoming." Felix detested that he was the only lead, and he was blind to his own twin. "We've got to take him out before he gets here. He's not as dangerous as a rogue, but he's still a threat—not only to Harmony but also to the clan."

"We might have bigger issues then Henry. The Texas clan sent us a message this morning, they want Tex returned within forty-eight hours or they will come to fetch him."

Felix moved around the sofa to sit across from Ty. "I thought Tex explained he didn't wish to return and that he wanted to stay here in Alaska. It's his right to change clans, especially with the abuse he suffered under the Alpha."

"Normally, yes, but according to Avery, Tex gave up that right when he became a member of the guard."

"What? I've never heard of that before. Can he do that? Can he force Tex back to Texas?"

Ty dragged his hand through his shoulder-length black hair. "Clans years ago used to do it, to protect their secrets. But to answer your question, no, we won't force Tex to go back. I've sent Robin to question him about it, and Raja is with her."

"Where's Tabitha?"

"Adam took her to visit Bethany. The women are online shopping." Ty visibly shivered as if shaken by the idea. "If I never have to go shopping with them again, it will be a blessing. Women take forever to pick out what they need. Men just go in, grab what we came for, and go."

Felix couldn't help but sympathize with that. He watched Tabitha and Bethany shop online together, and he could only imagine what it was like taking them out shopping where they could try everything on. It would have been a nightmare, especially with the constant threats to Tabitha's safety.

"Back to Henry, we believe he will come after Harmony alone, so for now we are going to wait until we know where he is before we plan any kind of attack. With Avery's newest threat, we can't spread the guards out dealing with multiple threats, especially not this close to Tabitha's announcement."

"Announcement?" Felix raised an eyebrow.

"The book alerted Tabitha that she's nearing the announcement and we should make some final preparations. We're waiting for something to happen before she comes out to all clans, but I believe it will be happening soon."

The book Ty spoke of was the one that was handed down Tabitha's line of tigers, and it would help her take her position as Queen of the Tigers. It had guided her to form a core group that had originally included only him, Marcus, and Thomas, but now had grown to include Adam, Shadow, and Styx.

"With both Adam and myself mated, and Korbin in Ohio as the Captain of Tabitha's guards, I'd like to promote a new member to the team."

Ty ran his hands over the thighs of his jeans and leaned forward. "Who?"

"Carran." The only black tiger of the clan, he had been proving himself as an amazing guard both in practice drills and on missions. He's young but would be a perfect fit for the team.

"I've heard our little black tiger is making a name for himself." Ty nodded. "With the increased threat, I've asked Taber to contact his brothers to see if one of them would come to guard Tabitha. A big bear by her side with you and Adam will scare some attack right from the start. Thaddeus has agreed."

Tad was the next oldest after Taber and Thorben and had been traveling between the compound and his family's island just off of Nome. He was nearly as good a guard as his older twin brothers, and he would be another great addition to Tabitha's guards. "It will be great to have Tad as part of the team. When does he arrive?"

"The youngest of the Kodiak Bears brothers, Theodore, will be delivering some additional custom furniture tomorrow, and Tad will fly in with him. Theodore has offered to stay on once he finishes his deliveries, if we could provide him a workshop. He'll join us next week if we still need him. The other Brown twins, Turi and Trey, will stay in Nome to protect their homeland with their father, but they will be available if we need them."

"Very well. Having Tad will allow us to have someone with Carran without Adam and me working overtime to train him. Tad knows what is expected, and I'm just down the hall in a guest room if anything comes up."

Ty leaned back against the sofa. "I know you've found your mate now, but that doesn't change that I want you in the building." Ty had a connection with each dedicated member of his clan, letting him know what was happening with each of them. Not to mention that he could smell the subtle changes in Felix's scent now that he found Harmony.

Felix nodded, he had already suspected that Harmony would have to join him in his one-room guest bedroom. While it was larger than her studio apartment, it would still be cramped for two people. "I understand."

"Raja and I were speaking of this very issue this morning. We've decided to get Ryan and his construction crew to add on to the main building. Plans are being drawn up now, and we're going to add a second floor. Tabitha and my quarters as well as Raja and Bethany's quarters will be in the middle with yours on the side of ours and Shadow's on the other side of Raja's. This will allow us all more privacy while keeping the mates safe. We'll have a private entry to the second floor so it will be out of bounds for anyone without permission. It will allow us all more room to grow, with mates and cubs as they come." Ty explained.

Felix nodded, excited about the possibility of moving out of the small room in the future. "It sounds like a logical plan and will allow the Captains of the Guards to be closer if anything should happen. What about yours and Raja's quarters now?"

"Adam and Styx will take them over. Having the seconds for each guard team close at hand will be additional protection. There's enough room for them to grow into it as well. So we won't have to worry about things for a while. We're also planning to turn one of the guest rooms down here into a living room so Raja and I could meet with the clan in a more homely setting without having them upstairs endangering the mates." Ty reached forward, grabbing his vibrating cell phone from the coffee table before looking back up at Felix. "Ryan and his men will work quickly and the bears have agreed to help. They should be able to finish the addition within three months, hopefully sooner. I'd prefer to have it done before Tabitha's announcement, but I'm not sure that will be possible."

"Tabitha will be safe either way. We'll see to that." It was stupid to tell his Alpha that, but he felt he had to. He wanted to make it clear that mating with Harmony wouldn't change his duty to protect Tabitha.

"I know we will. Now what about your mate? You said she wished to speak with me. Why don't we go find her and see what I can do for our newest tigress?" Ty rose from the sofa.

Felix followed his lead, tingling with anticipation to get back to his mate. He wasn't used to having someone he felt so connected to, the need to be with her so strong it was almost overpowering. The beast within him growing impatient to claim her as his, clawing at his insides and demanding to take over.

* * *

Harmony was bent over blow-drying her hair, her fingers combing through the red strands of wet hair, when Felix returned. Looking up, she found Ty standing beside him. She looked down at herself, thankful that she dressed in jeans and a tank top after stepping out of the shower instead of just keeping the towel around her until her hair was dry.

She shut off the blow dryer and laid it on the dresser. "I didn't expect you to come here, I thought…" She ran her fingers through her still-damp hair hoping to make herself somewhat presentable.

"Felix and I finished, and it just made more sense for us to come to you instead of him coming back to escort you to us." Ty stood there, his thumbs hooked through the belt loops of his jeans.

So we're back to me being escorted from place to place, a prisoner again. Before she could complain, Ty added, "I see the concern in your eyes. I only meant you haven't been to my quarters so you'd need help finding it. Now, how about we sit, and you tell me what you wanted to see me about." Ty motioned to the small seating area.

She nodded, making her way to the sofa, hoping that Felix would sit next to her. Ty took the chair across from her, and Felix hung back. "I asked to meet with you for a couple reasons, but something was brought to my attention this morning that I think needs to be approached first. Robin is sharing in my nightmares. She's seeing what happened before. Adam believes it's because of the connection she shares with me, and I wanted to speak with you. I thought it might be best if I mentioned it first since it's because of me. Is there anything you can do to help her?"

Ty leaned back against the chair, his hands crossed over his stomach looking relaxed while his gaze on her was all business. "The connection for her is going to be different since she's human, but I will work with her and teach her how to block them. However, it's going to be a learning curve for all of us. Your connection and loyalty to Robin is what you should have with an Alpha. It's never happened with a human before."

"Would it help if I was committed to an Alpha? To you?"

A hint of amusement sparked in his eyes. "Are you committing to the clan? Is that what you want?"

Damn it, she knew he'd ask that. She wasn't ready to make that commitment unless it would help Robin. After everything Robin did to help her, Harmony couldn't leave her suffering. "If I'm going to be mated to Felix, I don't have much choice, do I? I also care about Robin, and I don't want her to suffer because of my shit."

Ty looked at her seriously. "We'd never force the clan on you. However, being Felix's mate and his position within the clan, yes, it would be better for everyone involved if you were committed to the clan. We're not sure how that will affect the bond between Robin and you. I believe there will be little to no change. However, if Robin were ever against what I've decided for the clan, then you would suffer with the confliction. It could ease the affect it's having on Robin, but I doubt it. I believe you'll still be more bound to Robin than to me."

She had hoped that it would help Robin more, but it would at least make things easier for Felix once they were mated. More for her to think about and weigh. She wasn't ready to commit tonight. Ty seemed like a good Alpha, but she been down that path before—and it landed her in Henry's claws. "I was hoping that if I committed to you and the clan that it would ease things for Robin. I never realized reaching out to her would cause this bond. She's only human—it's too much for her."

Ty nodded. "If I had known the extent of the affect, I would have tried working with her before. I'll meet with her when I'm done here to see what can be done. Her connection to the clan is strong, so I should be able to give her at least some help. Her issue is that she's human, when this happens with an Alpha, the shifter is already designed to separate things so that feeling the clans emotions doesn't overwhelm you or divert your attention away from what needs to be done. Back to you committing to the clan…is that something you're planning to do?"

Felix shifted his weight from one leg to the other, drawing her attention. "Harmony, don't do this because of the mating. Devoting yourself to the clan is a bigger decision than that. We'll work things out whatever you decide."

"I'll be honest: I'm not ready to make the commitment to the Alaskan Tigers or to any clan for that matter. I don't want to push myself back into the situation I was in before in Ohio." Ty cleared his throat as if he wanted to say something. "If I could finish…with that being said, I respect the clan and will do nothing to harm what you have here. I'm concerned that my presence is going to bring trouble to your doorstep. I appreciate all that you and the clan are doing for me, and I believe I will be ready to make the commitment if I can just have a little more time."

Ty nodded and looked toward Felix before turning back to her. "We are nothing like the Ohio clan. Actually, we found out another clan is abusing its members, and we are taking action to stop it. However, I realize that you need to see it, not be told that. I won't force the clan on you, but you have to realize that without your commitment, there's going to be limitations to your presences there. Such as what Felix can tell you about the clan's activities."

"I know, but I also know that he won't be able to tell me a lot of things, anyways. His position in the clan will always be above mine. I'm not strong enough to reach his position in the clan, even if I had centuries to do so. Years ago I realized I'm a weak shifter, and nothing's going to change that." She looked toward Felix, her lips curved down in a frown. "I'm sorry."

Felix stepped around the coffee table to the sofa, reaching out for her hand as he sat down next to her. "There's nothing to be sorry about."

Ty smirked, leaning forward. "Actually, our clan is a bit different than others. We realize that keeping secrets from your mate is difficult, causing strain within the mating. Mates of the guards are allowed to attend most meetings. In most cases, things are not kept completely confidential between mates, but outside of the mating, nothing can be shared. Now, there are exceptions to this, but this is normally the case. With your commitment to the clan, it would allow you to attend things with Felix, to know what is happening within the clan as well as concerning the clans and its members. Without it you won't be able to attend, nor will he be able to speak about it. This includes some developments on Henry."

Developments on Henry—but that's concerning me. "That's a little close to blackmail for my tastes."

Ty shook his head, a clump of his dark hair coming loose from behind his ear. "Not blackmail, I'm just stating the facts. There could be developments on the search for Henry that affect things beyond you. He might be after you, but he also has history with Felix and the clan. After the earlier phone call, I believe part of his fascination with you is because you're to be Felix's mate."

She couldn't believe what she was hearing. Ty was using her desire to know what was happening when it came to Henry to get her commitment to the clan. It reminded her a little too much of the Ohio Alpha and his deceiving techniques to get someone to do what he wanted. Was Ty the same way? Or was he truly just trying to let her know what would happen?

She dug her nails into the palm of her hand, trying not to show that she was disappointed. "The other reason I asked to speak with you was because I wanted to help Connor and Lukas go through the information they've found. I know Robin has been doing it, but she's doing too much. I guess based on your last comment that wouldn't be possible."

Once again Ty shook his head, confirming her original thought. "I'm afraid not. They're working on more than just Henry, and some information they find might pertain to something else as well. Robin has been helping Connor because of her computer skills."

"I'm tech savvy. I might be able to help." This time she wasn't able to keep the disappointment and anger from her voice.

"Harmony, I understand how you feel, but without your commitment, I can't risk our other endeavors. If things change in the future, I know Connor would be honored to have your assistance. Connor and Lukas are overworked, but at this time, there's no one else to help them besides Robin." Ty rose. "If that's all, I should check in with Robin before I find my mate."

She rose, remembering that he could possibly be her Alpha in the future, but even if he wasn't, he was still Felix's and he deserved respect. "Thank you. I appreciate you coming, I'll let you know my decision soon."

"Felix, if I could have a moment of your time before I leave…outside." Ty strolled to the door, expecting Felix to follow.

Seeing him out, she realize she had a number of decisions to make. Either she wanted to be a part of this clan—Felix's family—or she didn't. If she didn't, how would that affect her mating with him? If she did commit to the clan, how would it affect Robin? She hated that she had more than just herself to think about. Her decisions now affected not only her, but also Felix and Robin. A human caught up in the shifter world because she mated with Adam.

Chapter Six

Felix quietly followed Ty out and across a small patch of grass until they were out of hearing range even for a shifter. "Everything okay, Ty?"

"Harmony is still questioning her loyalties. I know it's going to make you claiming her more difficult, but you have to watch what you tell her. Any confidential information that you share with her could be used against her if she chooses to leave us." Ty looked around to make sure no one was close enough to overhear them. "You can't mention Tabitha coming out as Queen of the Tigers. We can't let that get beyond the Elders yet. Not even to the clan, not yet. That also means until we know where she stands I don't want her in the main building. She's too much of a loose cannon right now."

He wasn't sure he liked the term 'loose cannon' describing his mate. "Loose cannon?"

"When someone has gone through substantial abuse and then they feel safe, they will sometimes fall apart. Harmony went through months of torture and abuse, now she finally has people that will catch her if she falls. It could only be a matter of time before she has a major meltdown." Ty dragged his hand through his hair, tugging the strands away from his face. "To be honest, I'm surprised she's accepted you like she has."

"Me, too, but I think you're underestimating her. Robin thinks she's making real progress—she's even agreed to have lunch with the women tomorrow."

"She's making progress, I can see that, but she's also having the nightmares still. She's living through it night after night in her dreams. I just want you to be prepared that she could slide back and lash out. Without her commitment to the clan, I can't risk what information she could gain."

"I understand." He did, but with his Alpha's new orders, it was going to make him claiming her even more difficult. Once the mating had started, he wouldn't be able to keep himself away from her, and he couldn't be in the main building doing his job and with Harmony at the same time.

As if Ty read his mind, he added. "Once your mating has started you'll be responsible if you bring her to the main building, and I don't want her there while you're guarding Tabitha. Not until we are sure where things stand with her." Ty strolled away, leaving Felix standing in the cool night air lost in his thoughts.

Would Harmony have a breakdown now that she had people to support her? Would it force the wedge between them again? Was all the progress they had made for nothing? The amount of unanswered questions that ran through his mind was annoying, not the mention the doubt that was now creeping back in.

He turned on his heels, heading back to her. There was no better time to start working on making their mating official. Stepping inside, he found Harmony pouring a glass of iced tea. Slipping up behind her, he slid his arms around her waist. He had been dying to do that since he walked in, now there was nothing stopping him. Nuzzling against the base of her neck, he took a moment just to breathe in her essence, the strawberry cream shampoo had him pressing his nose further into her hair. "I don't want you binding yourself to the clan because of me."

"It's not just you, there's Robin as well. More importantly, you know what happens with solitary shifters if they don't go true rogue—they are easy prey to others. I don't want to be without a clan completely, and I'm not strong enough to handle being prey and winning in a fight against others." She rested her head against his and laid her hands over his.

"You won't be alone. I'll be by your side."

Wriggling around in his arms, she turned to face him. "Felix, you can't honestly stand there and say that if I left your clan you'd leave with me."

"You're my mate." He hated to think of the idea of leaving his clan—they were his family. He had worked too long and too hard to earn the position he did to give it all up, but what choice would he have? His beast would choice their mate over his clan.

Leaving out a deep sigh, she looked into his eyes. "Fine, let's put it this way, you can't say you would follow me without hating me for it."

"Harmony, why are we having this discussion? Do you want to leave Alaska?" His heart beat a little faster at just the thought. Would she really leave the sanctuary she found?

"No. I mean, I don't know. Can this ever really be my home? They know what happened with Henry. Plus, being here is only bringing danger to your clan. Damn it—I don't want to be under another Alpha like my last."

"Ty is nothing like that. I've been with him since he took over the clan, working closely with him. He's the one that gave me the opportunity to prove myself by guarding him. When he mated, he asked me to be the Captain of Tabitha's guards. There's no higher honor than that, besides Raja's position as Lieutenant." He ran his hand up her back. "No one knows except Robin, Ty, Raja and their mates. It's not like everyone knows your past. Not that it's important—everyone has a past—but this can be your family if you just allow us in."

He wanted her to commit to the clan so he wouldn't have to choose between the two things that meant the most to him. Maybe taking Henry out of the equation would help her feel a little less hesitant. Ty's words begin to replay in his mind. Did he suspect that Harmony might try to leave the clan? Is that why he didn't want her helping Connor when they desperately needed the assistance?

He took a deep breath and asked the question looming on his mind. "If we weren't mates, would you leave the clan?"

"I don't know. I like it here. Robin, Tabitha, Bethany, and Kallie are quickly becoming friends, and I've never had someone I've considered a friend. I've never heard of another clan where the Alpha Female and Lieutenant's mate actually mingle with the clan members. So many other clans have this great divided between the Elders and the clan members. There's no true family as the one I've witnessed here. Ty is accepting enough to allow bears and a wolf into the compound, which is almost unheard of."

"Then why doubt Ty? You trust Robin, and she's committed to the clan. Why do you want to run from it when it can give you so much more than you've had in the past? I'd like to think you know I wouldn't lead you into anything dangerous, yet you run from the people I consider my family." Felix's fingers played along the edge of her tank top. He wanted to let his hands explore her body, but the conversation they were having was more important so he forced his beast to wait again.

She ran her hands along the front of his chest. "Because it scares me. Everything I've ever known is so different. My past proves Alphas aren't like Ty. To trust another and put myself in that situation again is daunting. Don't you think I wish I could just make the commitment—to take the doubt of the whole situation out of your eyes and to be able to give back to the clan and help find Henry? I would if I could, but the unknown is terrifying."

His fingers eased up the tank top revealing a little more skin, teasing along the bare flesh. "Let me claim you as my mate, and you will feel my connection to the clan. You'll know what I've gone through in the past with them and the love that we share. There will no longer be any doubt when it comes to committing."

"You're using that to mate me?"

He pressed his head closer to her neck, nibbling along the tender flesh where her neck and shoulder meet. "You know we're going to mate. Why push it off when it can help you gain more confidence in the clan and give you everything you've searched for?"

"How do you know what I've searched for?"

He drew his tongue along the spots he just nibbled at before answering her. "I know what we all want. We all want to find our mate because it completes us. Can you honestly say you don't want this mating? A clan to call home—one that is nothing like what you know but is a true family?" When she remained silent, he continued. "I thought so."

"I can't—not yet, I need more time." Even as she said it, her body betrayed her, her fingers pulling his T-shirt from his jeans until she had enough room to slide her hands under the thin material.

It was no surprise that she was going to fight the mating at every turn. He only hoped he could convince her before the mating desire set in, bringing the painful longing for their mate's touch with it.

* * *

With the covers drawn tightly around Harmony, she laid there mentally kicking herself for not giving in to her beast. The tigress wanted Felix and was growing more and more impatient with her delays. Her heated body felt like someone took a flame and glided it over her skin, warming her, it was the beginning of the mating desire she'd heard so much about and would only grow worse the longer she refused Felix. She couldn't complete the mating until she was certain things were going to turn out.

Having the connection to Henry through his bite mark on her thigh, could she work it so he knew where she was? She absently ran her hand over the scar. If she knew he left Ohio, it might be possible for him to know she left the compound. Slipping off the bed, she formed the plan to go after Henry herself. This wasn't the Alaskan Tigers' fight; it was hers. If she was going to be a clan member then she needed to take responsibility and not bring problems to the clan gates.

Pulling on her jeans again, she grabbed the hip holster that Felix brought earlier, sliding the gun into it. One magazine is all she had, but she'd make each bullet count. If she died before she could eliminate Henry, she could only hope that he left the clan alone.

Gathering a few things, she stuffed them in the small duffle bag. Sneaking off the compound wasn't going to be easy, but she'd give it her best shot. She hooked her fingers in the thick curtain material, easing it back to not cause attention and still allow her room to peer out. Not surprisingly, she found guards circling the perimeter, securing the compound. Day and night, they always seemed to be on duty, and there never seemed to be less, even in the middle of the night.

The ground was lighted with the evening lights, making it easy for the members to see as they went about their evening activities, many of them out for their nightly runs. Later, the lights would be dimmed while most of the clan slept, with only the guards moving about the grounds. She'd wait a little longer until it was at its darkest. Then she could use the night to conceal her as she made her way across the compound and up the fence to the other side.

Once she was beyond the walls of the compound, she'd figure out a way to get a message to Henry. She'd find him if he didn't find her first. It was time to take her life back into her own hands. She couldn't commit to a mate and a clan while she worried about placing everyone around her in danger.

Chapter Seven

Felix awoke with a start, his heart beating against his ribcage and his whole body screaming something was wrong. He opened his shields to check on Ty and Tabitha just down the hall. They were safe and sleeping peacefully. Lying there, listening to the ear transmitter, everything seemed calm. He laid there after coming to the conclusion that it had to be a dream, his eyes drifting shut when his phone rang. *Adam.* He's not on guard duty with Tabitha. What the hell had Adam calling?

Sliding his finger over the answer button, he brought it to his ear. "Hello."

"I need you here. Robin is freaking out. You need to get over here now." The alarm thickened Adam's voice.

"I'll be right there." Jumping out of bed, he ended the call. It had to be about Harmony.

He slipped into the jeans and shoes that he always kept close to the bed for emergencies before slipping on a T-shirt. Grabbing his shoulder holster, he charged out the door. There wasn't a minute to spare if something was wrong with his mate. He set off in a steady jog until he made it outside, then he ran through the night almost at tiger speed. Thoughts of what could have happened raced through his mind. He knew no one was on the compound grounds, so Henry couldn't have made it this far yet.

Skidding to a halt in front of Adam's cabin, he sent dirt flying through the air. He jumped onto the porch as Adam pulled open the door. "What's going on?"

"Inside." Adam nodded.

Felix stepped around him, and Robin came into view. She sat on the sofa, the cinnamon and spices from the tea she was clutching drifted toward him. Her eyes looked haunted and full of regret. What had happened since he retired for the evening?

"Oh, Felix, you're here." Tears fell down her cheeks, but he wasn't sure if they were tears of pain or gratitude.

"What happened?" Felix moved in, coming to sit across from her but leaving the comforting to her mate who would do a better job at it.

"Harmony. Oh, Felix, you have to help her. She's gone!" She cried out as Adam wrapped his arm around her shoulder, comforting her.

"What?" Felix nearly jumped from the chair. "I just saw her—she was tired and going to bed. What do you mean 'she's gone'?"

"I was asleep, thrilled that I wasn't sharing one of her dreams again. I thought maybe the tricks Ty taught me this afternoon were working. When I woke, I realized why I wasn't having her nightmare—she's not sleeping." With shaking hands, she reached out to set the tea mug aside. "I can feel her, but she's left the compound. She's determined to take Henry down herself instead of bringing the danger to the clan. You have to do something."

"Where is she?" Felix could kick himself for not seeing it earlier. After Ty delivered the news that she couldn't help with the search, she had gone quiet. He should have realized that she was working on plans of her own. Damn it—what kind of mate was he that he didn't even know she was planning something.

"She's got at least an hour head start on us. She's heading toward town, hoping to catch a ride," Robin explained, her head resting against Adam's chest.

Felix rose, he'd have to wake Ty and let him know before he could find his mate.

"I'm going with you."

"The hell you are, Robin!" Adam kept his arm around her, stopping her as she tried to stand from the sofa.

"I must go with Felix if we're to bring Harmony back. He needs me with him in order to find her." She ran her hand over Adam's leg. "If we both go, we have a better chance of bringing her back tonight and keeping her out of trouble."

"I'll find her myself," Felix told her. "Call me if you have any other information."

Robin laid her hand over Adam's, but her gaze was on Felix. "Henry is going to be drawn to her, knowing that she's alone. We have to bring her back tonight. In order to do that, you need me with you. I'll be able to feel her stronger as we get closer to her."

"I don't like the idea of my mate leaving the compound without me, but she's right. If you stand a chance of bringing Harmony back tonight, you need Robin with you." Adam kissed the top of Robin's head, sending a danger through Felix's heart at the display of love between them. "Don't discount my mate because she's human. She's a good shot, and with our mating, she's faster and stronger than the average human. She can hold her own."

"We can't both leave Tabitha unprotected," Felix told Adam, softening a little to the idea. He'd do whatever he could to find his mate quickly, including using his best friend's mate as a compass if he needed to. If Henry made it there before he could get the women back to safety, it was going to be tricky to protect both women.

"I know. Take Taber or Thorben with you. I trust them to help if things wrong." Adam dragged his fingers down Robin's arm. "If it was anyone else but you, I wouldn't agree to send my mate, but I know you'll protect her as if she was yours."

Felix nodded. "You have my word."

"Very well. I'll let Ty know. You get one of Kallie's mates and gear up. Robin will be ready when you are."

Robin turned her head, resting it in Adam's shoulder, her lips hovering above his neck. "Thank you."

"I'll get an SUV and be outside your cabin in twenty minutes." With that, Felix took two quick strides to the door. With one final look back at the couple, he opened it. *Damn Harmony for not only risking herself but the people that had come to care about her.*

Felix headed to recruit Taber for the newest mission, but the command center caught his attention and raised his anger. Whoever was on duty wasn't doing their job if Harmony was able to sneak off the grounds without raising alarm. It would add a few minutes to the lead Harmony had on them, but if the compound was going to be safe, he needed to stop there and drill a few lessons into whoever was behind the cameras. Tonight it was someone sneaking off, but next time it could be someone attacking the compound.

He pushed the door open, ready to tear someone's head off. Felix was shocked to find Mike sitting behind the computer station, cup of coffee in hand. Mike was one of the most dedicated on command-center duty. It was unlike him to let someone slip in or out of the compound.

"Felix, what can I do for you?" Mike asked, sitting his coffee aside.

Taking a deep breath, Felix's jaw set. "We had someone leave the compound under the cover of night. I want to know how it happened."

"Who? When?" Mike turned back to the monitors, scanning them again.

"Harmony, about an hour ago. I want to know how it happened and where, and I want to know now."

Mike shot a quick look over his shoulder back to Felix. "Are you sure? I haven't seen any unusual movement."

"Damn right I'm sure. She's not here. I want to know how you managed to overlook her climbing a fence." Felix slammed his hand against the door, splintering it.

"Felix." He turned to find Ty coming up the stairs. "Go find her. I'll deal with Mike, and we'll figure out how this happened."

"If someone can leave the compound unnoticed, someone can get in. Tabitha's in danger if people aren't doing their job." Felix's nails dug into the palm of his hand.

"There are a few spots on the compound that the cameras don't cover. New cameras have arrived but have yet to be put up. The guards know of the spots, and they monitor them closely," Mike defended. "I've been on duty and haven't left my post...I haven't seen anything, Felix."

"This is unacceptable." Felix's beast's attention was caught with the anger coursing through him.

"She was never a prisoner here—none of the members are."

Spinning toward his Alpha, a growl erupted from Felix. "She's my mate. If it was Tabitha, wouldn't you be angry?"

"If it was my mate, I'd be searching for her and figure out how the hell it happened later." Ty glared at Felix for a moment. "Harmony pointed out a flaw in our protection. She had time to study us. Anyone who's attacking won't be able to do that. We'll deal with adding more cameras and possibly more guards if needed, but now it's important that you find Harmony before Henry does."

His Alpha was right. He'd deal with Mike and whatever flaws laid in their security after he found his mate. "Fine." *Harmony, I'm coming for you.*

* * *

Creeping through the woods with the darkness covering it like a thick blanket had Harmony on edge. In the security of the compound over the last few weeks, she forgot how much she hated hiding in the woods, the darkness clinging to the trees and making the forest seem sinister. Occasionally, she'd catch a glimpse of the twinkling stars overhead, which eased the pulse rising in her throat.

If she'd shift, she could make the twenty miles from the compound to Fairbanks in less than an hour. But in her tiger form, the connection to Henry was stronger. With her shields down in tiger form, she couldn't block the connection as well. He'd pinpoint her location before she could get far enough from the clan to keep the danger away. The whole point of her running was to protect those she had come to care about. She couldn't risk them now, she'd have to continue the journey on foot. With luck on her side, she could make Fairbanks by morning.

A howl echoed from the top of the mountain, stopping her in her tracks. The wolves of the area didn't seem to like her being in their domain. They could smell her tigress but couldn't find it, all they could find was a human. Some humans would be scared off, but her beast only laughed that the wolves were on edge. She wanted to shift, to make the territory her own, just in spite. There was no time for games, though, not tonight.

She quickened her pace—she had to make it to Fairbanks in order to catch the eight o'clock flight to Seattle if she was to get away before Felix found her. Seattle would allow her the distance and crowd to hide from him. If their mating had been more conventional and he was able to feel her feelings even before the mating was complete as most were, she wouldn't have been able to slip off the compound grounds without him noticing.

Damn Henry for ruining everything! If it weren't for him, she'd have been able to claim her mate like she was destined to do. They'd share the bond that mates do from the start, but the bond with Henry was getting in the way of what she should have had with Felix. Eliminating him would put everything back to where it should have been and would give her the life she was destined to have—the life she didn't know she wanted until earlier that day. Now, she'd stand and fight for it with her dying breath.

Chapter Eight

Felix leaned against the black SUV in front of Adam's cabin waiting for Robin and Taber. He was eager to just jump into the SUV and drive off, leaving the others behind. However, the Alaskan Tigers were about teamwork, not going off half-cocked by yourself. Taking a deep breath, he filled his lungs with the night air, catching teases of his mate's scent before letting it out slowly. He needed to keep himself and his beast under control if he was going to keep his head in the game.

Adam came out of the cabin, his arm tightly around Robin's waist. "I'm trusting you to protect my mate and bring her back just as she is now."

"She'll be safe, you have my word." Felix nodded to Adam, knowing that, even with the bond between them, sending his mate off the compound without him was difficult. "Robin, are you armed?"

"Yes." She pulled her lightweight jacket back to reveal the gun riding just in front of her hip. "I have a knife strapped to my ankle as well."

"Very well. We're just waiting for Taber, and then we're ready." Felix pushed off the SUV and stood straight. "Adam, I've asked Theodore to cover my guard duty in the morning. He'll meet you at Alpha's quarters. Hopefully we won't be longer than that."

"Don't worry, I have it covered. Tabitha will be protected." Adam turned Robin into his body, wrapping both arms around her. It was as if he was trying to stock up on the attention so that when she was gone he wouldn't feel as alone.

"Thorben and Tad are available if anything comes up," Taber stated, coming around the front of the SUV.

"The clan will be fine. You need to focus on finding Harmony and bringing everyone back safely." Adam kissed the top of his mate's forehead. "Be safe and listen to Felix. If he says run, you run. Don't question him. I want you back here uninjured."

Robin pulled back enough to look up at her mate. "Don't worry, I'll be fine. I'm not going to do anything stupid." She leaned up to kiss him.

Felix couldn't stand the intimacy any longer, not when his mate was out there alone. He did the only thing he could in that moment, he turned around and headed to the driver's side. Taber followed, taking the passenger's side. It would give the mates a moment of privacy before Robin climbed into the backseat.

He was determined to get Harmony back and convince her she was his mate before anything else could happen. Giving her time to accept him was great in theory, but it also left things incomplete, including the mating bond. She'd never again be able to hide something so big from him…their bond would ensure that.

"We'll find her." Taber's deep voice pulled Felix out of his thoughts.

"What?" Felix looked over at Taber.

"You're putting indents in the steering wheel." Taber nodded to the wheel that Felix held in a death grip. "I know you're worried about Harmony."

Felix took a deep breath and loosened his grip on the steering wheel. "I know we will, and when I get my hands on Henry, I swear I'll make him suffer for everything he did to her—for causing this rift between us. His connection to her is why the bond isn't already there—the reason I didn't know she had this planned. Damn him!"

"We'll deal with him, but first we've got to get your mate back to safety. Then, if you want, we'll go after him. Do you know where he is?"

Felix shook his head. "Not yet. He's closer than he has been, but all I know for sure is that he hasn't made it to Alaska. There's something about the glimpse that I caught that makes me believe he's in Colorado, but I'm not sure." The back door opened, and Robin slid in. Felix turned to meet his partner's gaze. "She'll be back soon."

"Be safe," Adam told them before turning his attention back to his mate. "I love you."

Felix turned the key, bringing the engine to life before gazing back at Robin in the rearview mirror. "So where to?"

Robin scooted to the middle seat, positioning herself between Taber and Felix. "She's slinking through the woods, heading to Fairbanks. Take the road towards Fairbanks. Once we're closer, we're going to have to do the rest on foot."

Steering the SUV toward the main compound gate, Felix could suppress the anxiety of taking Robin on this mission. "I don't like the idea of taking you to traipse through the woods."

Robin leaned forward between the seats. "Unless you want to wait until she makes it to Fairbanks, I don't see any other option."

Felix could think of at least two different options, but neither of them seemed like a better decision. After all, he needed her to find Harmony quickly. Traipsing around the woods in the middle of the night was dangerous enough. Most animals would stay away from them once they caught the scent of their beasts, but having Robin with them would slow them down. She didn't have the night vision that Taber and he had, so they'd have to lead her through the woods if she was going to come out uninjured.

"She's about half-way to Fairbanks and less than a half-mile in from the road. There's a wolf stalking her from a distance, and it's making her uneasy." Robin leaned back, her eyes closed. "She's doing this for you—for you and for the clan. If she can take out Henry without bringing danger to the clan, she'll feel like she can finally accept you as her mate, to truly be a part of our clan."

"Damn it, she didn't need to do this to be a part of the clan! She is a part of us because she's my mate." Hitting the main road, Felix put his foot down on the gas, closing the distance between him and his mate.

"She didn't want to bring any more danger to Tabitha or the clan. There's been too much lately. Now that Pierce has been eliminated, there was hope that the clan could relax before taking on the next challenge, but she came along and brought more danger."

Taber turned in his seat, looking back at Robin. "Wait, how does she know about Pierce?"

"I told her," Felix explained, not taking his eyes from the road. He had done it before Ty expressed his desire to keep the clan's business confidential until Harmony decided where her loyalties lay. "She was concerned we wouldn't find Henry. Trying to lessen her fears, I told her that we had the best people available working on his location. That Connor was amazing with his computer skills, and we'd find him, just like we did with Pierce. She had to know this wasn't our first rodeo and that we'd find him before he could get to her."

Silence filled the car. It was almost as if they knew there were many more battles in the future of the Alaskan Tigers before they'd be truly safe. Even without the threat of Henry, there was still the Texas Tigers and Avery that posed a threat. With Tabitha's upcoming announcement as Queen of the Tigers, more threats could be waiting on the horizon. Only time would tell what was in store for the clan.

Felix's cell phone vibrated in his shirt pocket. He pulled it out, sliding his finger over it to answer before putting it to his ear. "Hello?"

"She went over the fence near the creek. There isn't a camera there. It's one of the unmonitored spots that will be addressed, but there's footage of her going down by the creek. Mike didn't think it was unusual since she's been spending a lot of time down at the creek over the last few weeks," Ty told him, a shuffle of papers in the background let Felix know he was still working.

Felix knew Harmony enjoyed the creek, especially the little hiding spot she made for herself, so he couldn't blame Mike for not finding it suspicious. "I appreciate you finding out. When I return, I'll go over any unmonitored area of the perimeter with Mike, and we'll secure them. If Harmony can leave that way, it's possible an enemy might use it to attack."

"I'd have had the information to you sooner, except something came up. Hold on." There was a mumble as Ty spoke to someone else, and more papers were shifted before he came back on the line. "Korbin called. Randolph sent a message asking for any of the Ohio shifters loyal to him to meet him in the spot they've held their meetings. Korbin and Jinx are trying to find out where, but so far they've had ten members leave the clan."

"Ten members? The clan only had twenty members to begin with. How much did Randolph have his hands in?"

"From what Korbin has gathered so far, the Alpha and Randolph have been preaching the need to kill Tabitha. It seems as though Randolph will be leading a small clan of his own—the rogues by his side—with the main goal of killing Tabitha." The anger seeped into Ty's voice.

It was insane that a group of tiger shifters wanted to kill Tabitha when everyone believed that if she was killed before her line could continue, the tiger shifters would cease to exist. Why would they want to kill off their own kind? None if it made sense to him.

"We knew there'd be opposition to Tabitha, especially once she comes out at Queen. This changes nothing. Any idea where Randolph is?" Felix careened around the corner quickly, sending Robin toward the door.

"I suspect he's in Ohio, but Connor is on it. There's a hit that Henry is in Colorado. He bought a ticket to Seattle, leaving tonight. Does that mean anything to you?"

Seattle? "No, should it?"

"I don't know. It means nothing to us, and no lead was found as to why. If he were coming for Harmony, why wouldn't he fly into Fairbanks? Or into one of the other airports in Alaska if he didn't want to deal with Border Control while crossing in and out of Canada?" Ty's confusion mixed with the anger.

"Stop," Robin called from the backseat.

"I've got to go." Felix slid the SUV to the shoulder.

"Find her and bring her home," Ty added before ending the call.

Putting the SUV into Park, he turned to Robin. "This is where she is?"

Robin nodded. "About a half-mile in from the road. She made exceptional time for staying in her human form. The longer we wait, the more distance she puts between us. Let's go."

"Won't she smell us coming?" Taber drew his hand through his shaggy hair.

"We'll have to stay downwind from her if we're to get to her without her smelling us first." Felix pushed open his door, his steel-toed boot hitting the cement as he lowered his legs to stand. The road was quiet, no animals scampering though the woods. The scent of Harmony's tigress had sent them scattering. To add his tiger and Taber's bear into it would scare off any remaining wildlife.

Robin stepped out, coming to stand next to him while buttoning her lightweight jacket. "I agree. We go downwind of her, but when we get close, you'll need to let her smell you. She's spooked and has a gun. I don't want any of us at the wrong end of it and end up with a bullet hole for our troubles."

"I'll go first. Stay close, and, Taber, you're in charge of protecting Robin. If anything happens, get her back to the SUV and get her to safety." Felix tossed the spare keys to Taber who was coming around the front of the SUV.

Taber caught the keys midair. "You hear that, Robin? You're stuck with me."

"We can't just leave you if something goes wrong," Robin tried to reason.

He spun toward Robin. She was a foot shorter than him, yet she had enough spitfire of someone twice her size. "I'll be fine, but I promised Adam I'd bring you back safe. Now if you're going to argue, I'll have Taber take you home now." When she remained silent, he nodded. "With that settled, let's go."

He led the way into the woods, knowing that Taber would take up the rear so Robin was in between them for additional protection. Entering the dark woods, he heard a faint click from behind him, and a pin light reflect off the ground. Turning, he found Robin holding a small pen-sized flashlight in her left hand. Her gun hand was free in case she had to go for it.

"What? I don't have the same freaky night vision you two have."

He couldn't help but smile. Robin had only been with the clan a few months, but she fit in like she had always been there. The easy nature she had with him proved she was truly part of the family. Shaking his head, he turned back around, heading deeper into the woods. He was able to pick up a whiff of his mate. The scent drifting to his nose was like a direct line to his shaft and nearly made him stumble over a log on the ground.

His beast charged forward, claws digging into his insides as if fighting to be released. Taking a deep breath, he tried to push his tiger down, but all it did was fill his body with her essence and make his tiger more anxious. They were pushing the limits of their beasts, denying this mating. The time he had to find her and get her back to the compound before his tiger would no longer be suppressed was narrowing by the second.

Taber stepped up next to him. "You haven't claimed her yet."

Felix looked to him, trying to decide if it was merely a statement or a question. Even in the dim light of Robin's flashlight he could see the questions in Taber's eyes. "I was giving her time to accept it. Tonight, almost…damn it, that's why she pulled away tonight."

Earlier in her studio, he thought he'd finally get to claim his mate, but she pushed him away, claiming she was tired. She knew then she was going after Henry, and he didn't even suspect it. How could he be so blind to his mate?

"The pain is going to set in soon if you don't. She might already be suffering from it." Taber whispered, keeping his voice low so Robin didn't hear him even though she was right behind them.

"What's going on? Something wrong?" Robin inquired, scanning the woods.

"Everything's fine. Let's go." Felix stepped over the log he almost tripped over, double-timing it in the direction of his mate. He wasn't sure he could even slow down if he had to. The beast within him controlled him more then he should have allowed.

Chapter Nine

Pain had tingled along each of her nerve endings since Felix left her apartment that night. If that wasn't bad enough, waves of horrific agony now coursed through her, doubling her over with each hit. Chills shook her body, making it hard to walk. The mating desire hit her full force, and there was no end in sight. She'd never make it back to the compound like this, nor did she suspect she could make the last few miles to Fairbanks. She'd suffer until her beast turned on her, driving her insane with need in the middle of the woods miles from her mate.

"Shit, can I do nothing right?" She collapsed onto a fallen tree, resting her back and head against a second tree covering it. Her heart beat so loudly in her ears that she couldn't even focus on where the wolf that was stalking her was. He had kept on her trail for the last few miles, watching her from a distance as if to make sure she left his territory.

A stick crunched twenty yards to her left, and she turned toward it, trying to get her eyes to focus. She also tried to smell whatever lingered in the shadows, but she couldn't get herself together enough.

Pushing away from the tree, she tried to get her legs to hold her weight. Not knowing what was there, she had no choice but to continue.

The pain stole her breath, but she wouldn't sit and die without at least trying. If she couldn't run, she at least had a weapon. She pulled the gun, trying to calm herself enough so that she wasn't shaking, and pointed it where the sound came from. "Don't come any closer or I'll put a hole in your ass!" She pulled the trigger, aiming just to the left of the noise to let whoever was there know that she was serious.

"Harmony, it's Felix." He stepped out of the clearing, his hands held out before him.

The sight of him stole her breath. She wanted to run to him, to feel his arms around her. More importantly, her tigress wanted to feel his hands on her body and his shaft buried deep within her. She might have gone to him if she didn't hear more leaves rustling as someone came up behind him. "Who's with you?" She aimed the gun slighting to the right of him, ready to take out whoever was behind him.

"Robin and Taber. We've come to find you," he explained as Robin stepped up next to him. Taber stayed a step in front of her, but Harmony could see his hand was still resting on his gun.

"Put up the gun, sweetie. No one is here to harm you. We came to find you, to bring you home." Robin tried to sooth her.

Harmony let out a sarcastic laugh, unable to stop it. "Then why's his hand on his gun?"

"Taber," Robin whispered.

"Taber is cautious. There's no telling what's in the woods with us. There's a wolf not thirty feet behind you, but he means you no harm. Now put the gun up, love." Felix stepped closer to her.

With each step her desire rose, and her hands shook. She took her finger away from the trigger, not wanting to shoot someone because she was shaking uncontrollably. "Felix." Even to her own ears, her voice held desire and need.

"It's okay, sweetie. I'm here now." He went to her, wrapping his arms around her.

"I wanted to go after him myself to keep you and everyone safe." She buried her face into his chest, breathing him in. "I'm sorry."

"Shhh, love. It's the mating desire. We have to get you back to the compound." He lifted her into his arms and nodded back to Taber and Robin.

"I'm in too much pain." His touch pushed the pain back, but it wasn't enough.

"I know. Just hang in there a few more minutes. We waited too long, that's why you're suffering now." He pressed his lips to her forehead. "We'll be back at the compound in a few minutes."

She wasn't sure she could last another second, let alone minutes to get back to the cabin. "Why am I in pain but you're not."

"I feel it as well, maybe not as strongly yet, but I was able to push mine down to focus it on finding you." Felix pressed her against his chest tighter before looking to Taber. "It's going to take longer then she has for us to get out of here unless you carry Robin."

"What?" Robin's eyes grew large as she looked at Felix and Harmony.

"Wrap your arms around his neck and your legs around his waist. We'll get out of here quick." When she stared at him in shock, he added. "It's either that or I claim Harmony here. It took us nearly ten minutes to get this deep into the woods, she doesn't have that long. Not unless you want her to go through agony. Your choice."

"He's right. We can make it out of here within a minute without having to keep our pace slow for you," Taber agreed drawing the attention to him.

"Please, Robin. I wouldn't ask if…" Pain tore through her, stealing her words.

Robin grabbed her stomach and nodded. "Fine. Just don't drop me."

"You're feeling her pain, too." Taber knelt before her so she could wrap her arms around his neck.

"Yes, but not as bad as before. The tricks Ty taught me must be working some." The pain was still clear in Robin's voice as she wrapped her arms around Taber's neck. "I don't know if I'll be able to hold on if the pain gets worse."

"We'll be back to the SUV before then." Felix took off with Taber falling into pace next to him.

"I'm sorry I've caused so many problems," Harmony whispered, placing her face against his neck.

"You haven't. Everything is going to be fine."

Felix's words did very little to comfort her. She wanted to be a part of the Alaskan Tigers, yet all she was doing was causing more problems. Poor Robin suffered with Harmony's emotions, nightmares, and pain. It seemed like all her life things had always gone wrong and that she had always made things worse when she tried to fix something. Would she ever be able to do something right?

* * *

Felix cuddled Harmony against him, his other hand resting on Robin's shoulder, trying to ease the women's pain while Taber drove like a mad man to get them back to the compound. It was all becoming too much, as they careened through the front gates. The moans of pain were quickly becoming screams of agony.

"Take care of your mate," Taber said as he skidded the SUV to a halt in front of Harmony's studio apartment. "I'll get Robin home to Adam."

"Update Ty." Felix flung the rear door open, slipping out of the SUV before reaching back in to grab Harmony. "Thank you both." He slammed the door shut just in time as Taber sped away.

"Felix…" Harmony cried out, her nails biting through his shirt.

"Almost." His desire practically buckled his knees. He wanted to take her right then. *Twenty steps, then you can claim her.* He took a deep breath and forced himself forward. Fumbling with the door handle, he cursed and finally managed to push it open.

He kicked the door shut, his lips finding hers. He backed her against the wall, turning her so that she was straddling his body with her back against the wall. His fingers wandered her body, and his mouth never left hers. Their tongues danced in each other's mouths, their beasts mixing growls with moans of desire. He trailed kisses down the length of her neck, his teeth nipping the soft skin where her neck and shoulder met.

* * *

The warmth of her place eased the chill and meant she could have Felix and the agony would finally be gone. "Felix, I need you." The mating desire was nearing its breaking point. She needed him now.

"I know, love." An arm wrapped around her waist, keeping her pressed against his body as he stepped away from the wall.

"Naked, now." She reached up for him, her fingers closing around the buttons of his jeans.

He tugged his shoulder holster off and sat it on the nightstand, placing his cell phone with it. "Give me your gun."

She slid her hip holster off, handing it to him with the gun still nestled safely inside it before turning her attention back to his jeans.

He pulled off his shirt, tossing it to the floor while she tugged down his zipper and slipped her hand inside the rough material. Her fingers wrapped around his shaft tearing, a growl from deep within him.

"Take these off." She slid his jeans down his hips.

"Only if you get naked." His fingers twisted around the material of her shirt, pulling it up and over her head. His beast was growing tired of waiting, wanting her body pressed against him. Yet he kept suppressing it, not wanting to rush the first time they'd make love.

"I thought you'd never ask." She teased, rising up enough to unbutton her jeans before sliding them down her legs. Suddenly, all her apprehensions were gone—thanks to the mating desire. Hopefully they didn't return with a vengeance later.

By the time she reached behind her to unhook her bra, Felix was out of his clothes. He pushed her down onto the bed, unhooking the bra himself as they fell back on the bed. In one quick movement it was unsnapped and off her body. His lips circled her nipple, grazing his teeth over it until her back arched into him.

"Felix, please," she moaned.

He tore his lips away from her breast, leaning up to look at her. "Please what? Do you want more? Less maybe?" Watching her, he waited for an answer.

"Felix!" His mouth on her breast felt so gentle and loving but suddenly sent horrific images through her mind of Henry's torture. She pushed against his chest. She couldn't do it. Not now, no matter how much agony she'd be in.

The moonlight peeked through the curtains, giving her the perfect glimpse of Felix, and her fears dissipated. All she could see was the man Felix was, not the man he reminded her of. Felix was her mate, completely different from his twin. This was her destiny, and she was going to claim it with both hands. She pushed the memories of her past away and pulled him to her. "Give me what I want, or I'll roll you over and take it."

"I'd just like to see that." He leaned over her, pressing his lips to hers for a soft kiss. When he pulled back, he let his lips hover just above hers. "Stop rushing me, I plan to enjoy this." He kissed her again, this time deeper, more passionately, stealing the breath from her.

He pulled his mouth from hers and kissed a path down her neck, breathing in the scent of his mate. Sensations collided and threatened to overwhelm him, but he pushed his beast away, trying to savor the moment.

He nodded, pressing his lips to hers. "You're mine for now and always." Laying her back, he kissed down her neck until he got to her breasts. Dragging his tongue in lazy circles around her nipples, he wanted her intently. Teasing her nipples gently, pulling them between his teeth until they stood to attention, he rested his weight on an elbow and used the other hand to explore the length of her body. Memorizing every curve.

He blazed a hot, wet trail of kisses across her stomach, stroking her thighs with his fingertips. With every touch, she arched her hips into him, demanding more. Desire coursing through him, he could wait no longer to claim her. His mind was in a sexual haze, and his beast was just below the surface, speeding the pace.

He spread her legs further, giving him the access he needed. With his control nearly maxed out, he was thankful she was wet because he had nothing left in him to go slow. He slid his shaft into her warm, wet core before pulling it back out and thrusting in again, his manhood filling her completely. He went as slow as he could the first few strokes so as not to hurt her, but with each stroke, the tempo intensified another level until his hips where slamming off her, driving the force with each pump. The thrusts became deeper and faster, falling into a perfect rhythm. Their bodies rocked back and forth, tension strained his muscles as he fought for the release he longed for.

"Felix!" Screaming his name, she arched her body into his as her release coursed through her, her nails digging into his chest and leaving deep welts and angry red scratches. He pumped once more and growled her name as his released followed.

He stayed perched over her with his shaft still buried deep inside of her, watching the afterglow fill her face. Her eyes were glossed over in ecstasy. The connection between them fully alive, her emotions were mixing with his, bringing a smile to his face. He collapsed onto the bed beside her and cradled her body tight against his, his fingers caressing her side in lazy strokes.

"I can feel your emotions." Her fingers trailed along his chest, brushing over the cuts from her nails. "Sorry about these, I didn't think I was that rough."

* * *

"It's heavenly to finally have that connection." He didn't add that if Henry hadn't tried to make her his that they would have had it before. "As for the scratches, don't be. I enjoyed the feeling of your nails digging into my chest."

He buried his face in her hair, the sweet honey scent from her shampoo teasing along his senses. "You're mine, and I love you." Pressing his lips to her forehead, he kissed her tenderly.

"I love you, too." She titled her head to look at him. "This connection between us—I never expected it to feel like this. I can feel everything. Your anger over Henry, hatred for the people who have brought danger to your clan, especially the rogues, but I can also feel the love for your clan as if it was my own. It's so much more than I ever expected."

"The clan is my family, as you are. If anyone messes with any member of the clan, I'd fight by their side. I'd stand for those who couldn't or shouldn't fight for themselves. Women and children of the clan are protected at all cost, and I'd fight their fight for them." He ran his hand along her arm. "You have to understand that I'd lay down my life to protect you and this clan."

She nodded. "I know—and it's admirable—but it scares me, too."

"Hopefully it will never come to it, but it's a risk you need to understand." His fingers traveled down the length of her body until he pulled away. Using his arms to hold him inches above her body, he took in the sight of his naked mate.

The scars that marred her body tore at his heart. He knew they were from the torture she endured at Henry's hand. The cuts along her sides had to be from knives since Henry had no claws. It took his mind a few moments to register the angry red burn across her stomach, just below her bellybutton. It looked like it was from a hot poker that someone would use in a fireplace.

"Don't." She rolled away from him and pulled the blanket over her.

"Harmony." He reached out for her, but she pulled further away.

"Don't. Just leave. I'd rather suffer with the mating desire then see pity in your eyes."

"I see what he did to you, and I hate myself, knowing that I could have stopped it. If I'd have done what I knew needed to be done years ago, none of this would have happened to you." He sank onto the bed, just beyond touching her. "It doesn't make up for what you went through, but I'm going to find him and make sure he's no longer a threat to you or anyone else. I'll see him dead for what he did."

"You couldn't have known this would happen. If my Alpha had been a true Alpha, he'd have never turned me over to him. This is more my fault then yours."

"How can you say that? You did nothing to deserve this."

She let her head fall back against the pillow. "You're half right— I did nothing."

"Oh, love." He reached for her, and this time she didn't pull away. Sliding his hand into hers, his thumb played gently over her knuckles. He fought the urge to pull her tight against his body and hold her there forever. "There was nothing you could have done. Though Henry cannot shift, he's still dangerous. Anything you'd have done would have only made things worse for you. It was your Alpha's responsibility to protect you, and he didn't."

"The burn was to teach me a lesson for trying to escape the first time. After that, things became worse. He was unpredictable. At some point, I realized that, if I didn't get out of there, he'd kill me." Her body shivered, but he suspected it wasn't from the chill so much as the memories being brought to the surface.

"It's okay." He moved closer to her, drawing her in across his chest. "I swear he'll never get his hands on you again. Unlike your former Alpha, I'll protect you."

"Right now, I just want to forget it all."

When she remained silent, he held her close, letting his eyes drift shut. Thankful to finally have claimed his mate, he laid there enjoying the moment because he knew it wouldn't last. Soon he'd have to find Henry and eliminate him if he wanted to keep his mate safe.

Chapter Ten

The sun was peaking around the curtains when Felix woke, Harmony still wrapped in his embrace. He never expected to spend the night at her place. He planned on moving into his room before they fell asleep, to be closer to Tabitha if anything should happen. With Henry flying into Seattle, he didn't have time to lay here cuddling with his mate. He needed to find out why Seattle. What was there that would make his twin go there?

"What are you thinking about?" Harmony's fingers teased along the lines of his abs.

"Work." He caressed along her spine, watching her. "We received word last night that Henry booked a ticket to Seattle. I need to get with the team and see if they figured out why Seattle."

She shot up, taking the sheet with her. She held the flimsy material over her breasts. "Seattle?"

He nodded. "Does that mean something to you?"

"It worked." She tugged the strand of hair out of her face. "I wasn't sure if it would, but it worked!"

He rose up on his elbow. "What the hell are you talking about?"

"I figured if Henry knew that I was here with you, I could get a message to him. I focused all my thoughts on Seattle, wanting to get him to meet me there. It was away from the clan, but close enough that I could get back to you quickly if I made it out alive."

"You were baiting him?" He glared at her, unable to believe what he was hearing. Was she insane? She had to be to bait someone that tortured her for months and threatened to kill her. Didn't she realize how dangerous Henry was? Or did the safety she had now distort all she went through?

"I had to if I wanted to find him. It seemed like a better idea than sitting around waiting for him to attack the clan. Damn it, Felix, I couldn't let him attack the compound. Not because of me. I couldn't bring the danger here with everything else that's looming. Don't you understand that?"

"You should have come to me. If we realized there was a chance you could convey a message to him, we might have set up a sting operation with you baiting him, but doing it yourself was dangerous. You could have gotten yourself killed." He ran his hand over his five o'clock shadow, feeling the stubble until he got his anger under control. "What matters is that you're safe. Get dressed. I have to let the Elders know."

"I think I'll stay here." She moved as if she was going to lie back down.

"Woman, you've got another thing coming if you think I'm leaving you alone. You're stuck with me until we have dealt with Henry, or that spot where you climbed over the fence is monitored.

You're not getting away again." He wasn't willing to risk the safety of his mate, even if he could now feel her emotions and plans as if they were his.

"I'm not going to do anything stupid. Go, I'll stay and keep the bed warm." She raised an eyebrow at him, letting him know she wanted him to make it quick so they could continue where they stopped.

"You're coming with me, and we'll be staying in my room from now on. I need to be close to the Elders in case of emergencies. You might want to gather your stuff now so we won't have to come back. Then we can go straight to my room and pick this back up." He scooted out of the bed, grabbing his boxers and jeans from the floor.

"At least can I shower?"

"Go ahead. I'll call Ty and have him gather the team. It will take a few minutes to get everyone together, but don't take long." He watched as she slipped from the bed and padded naked toward the bathroom. His shaft rose and his body screamed for him to follow her, but he knew where that would lead. They didn't have time, not with Henry already in Seattle.

A lump rose in his throat. For years he knew someday the time would come when Henry had to be eliminated, but now that the time was here, his emotions were all over the place. Anger that things had come to this, sadness for the knowledge if it wasn't him that killed Henry it would be one of the guards he was close to, and pity for Henry.

Even with everything playing havoc inside his mind, he knew without a doubt that he'd kill Henry without an ounce of hesitation. After what he did to his mate and the danger he was—not only to the clan and his mate, but to humans—there was no other options. It saddened him that it came to it, but there was no other recourse. He snatched his cell phone from the dresser and hit the speed-dial number for Ty.

"What's going on, Felix?" His Alpha's voice was strained, and if Felix wasn't mistaken, it sounded as if he had been up through the night, most likely trying to figure out the significance of Seattle before it was too late.

"Can you gather the team? I know why Seattle."

"Tell me why and I'll gather them."

Felix grabbed his socks and shoes and dealt with those as he filled in Ty. "Somehow she conveyed a message to him, letting him know she was going there. She wanted to get him away from the clan to keep you and Tabitha safe. He has to know that she's with me now because I've claimed her. It destroyed the connection he had with her. He'll come here, so we need to get a plan together."

"Speaking of the connection, I spoke with Robin this morning." Ty paused, there was some commotion on the other end. "Shit, Henry's on his way. Ten minutes conference room."

"Wait—what about Robin? Is she okay?"

"She's fine. I'll explain everything when you get here. I've got to get Raja and the rest of the guards." Without another word, Ty hung up.

What had happened when he claimed his mate? Did it make things worse for Robin? She experienced the pain of the mating desire, did she experience the mating as Harmony did?

* * *

Standing in front of the vanity, Harmony wiped the steam from the mirror to try to do something with the mass of red curls before Felix forced her to leave. Not recognizing the reflection, she did a double take. All her life she had been pale, the freckles and ruby red hair making her appear even more, but now her cheeks were rosy and full of color. There was now an impression of Felix's teeth on her shoulder where he broke the skin, claiming her.

"Wow!" She dragged her fingers through her curls, getting them out of her face so she could see it better. She couldn't believe the sudden changes in her appearance.

"Harmony, we should be going." Felix called from the doorway.

"Just give me another minute." She took a deep breath, pushing Felix's emotions away. His pain was tearing her insides apart and stealing her breath. Felix was being torn in different directions, and though he tried to hide it, it was eating at him. Leaning forward toward the mirror to add a little lip-gloss, she couldn't help but speculate that killing Henry himself would kill a part of her mate, no matter what he said. Would he still be the man she had come to trust and love over the last few weeks?

"Harmony."

"I'm coming." Did that man not have a patient bone in his body? A woman couldn't just jump out of the shower and into clothes. There was more than that to getting ready for a woman. She scrunched her curls one last time and looked over her appearance again. Her wardrobe was limited, so the jeans and pink tank top would have to work. On the way out the door, she'd grab her black sweater to keep the chill of the Alaskan air at bay.

Stepping out of the bathroom, she found Felix leaning against the doorway, looking slight impatient as he read something on his phone. "I'm ready."

He looked up from his phone, taking her in before letting out a deep breath through his teeth. "You look almost as good in clothes as you do naked beneath me. Looking at you there makes me think of the fun I could have stripping those clothes from your body with my teeth."

"We don't have time for that now." She grabbed her black sweater from the back of the chair and slipped into it.

"I could make time for it." He pushed off the wall and stalked towards her, desire seeping off him. "Right now I want nothing more than to forget about my duties even for an hour and toss you back on the bed and have my way with you." He was close enough to her now that she felt his warm breath against her face.

She laid her hand against his chest, feeling the contours under her fingertips. "Tonight. Right now the clan needs you, but there will be a lot of time for just us soon."

"Do you know something I don't?" He raised an eyebrow at her, as if to ask if she was planning something.

"Is it wrong for me to take some of your faith and believe things will work out?"

"You're not planning anything stupid, like leaving the compound without any support, are you? Because I'll have you lock in my room with guards watching your every move if you're even considering it." His slid his arms around her waist, pulling her close against his chest. "You mean too much to me for me to risk you."

"I have nothing planned, only to have your body next to me every night and to feel your shaft buried deep within me until I'm so sore I can't walk straight." She slipped the hand that was between them away, sliding it up his chest to rub the whiskers on his chin. "Now come on, we can't keep your Alpha waiting."

"You're right, but later you're mine." With his arm around her waist, he led her to the door.

As they stepped outside, the cool air gushed past her, chilling her to the core and freezing her wet hair in tiny ringlets. The tigress within her enjoyed the cold and even the snow, but her human form didn't have the same tolerance for the abrasive chill in the air. She tugged the sweater tighter around her as Felix pulled her closer to his body.

"Ty mentioned that there's a change in Robin's connection to you. Have you noticed anything different?" he asked, leading her down the walkway toward the main building where they would meet the team.

She took a moment to think about it before answering, but nothing felt anything different. "Nothing, but I've never been able to feel her emotions or anything. Only she suffered from my connection. I didn't realize what I did when I reached out to her. There was just something about her that made me believe I could trust her. I wanted to trust someone, so I reached out to her. I never meant to saddle her with my mess."

"Okay, we'll find out what he meant shortly." He opened the door, allowing her to enter the building before slipping his arm back around her waist.

"Felix," a deep, husky voice called.

Muscles tensed with alarm as a man stalked toward them. His short brown hair cut close to his head left his face in clear view, His eyes warned anyone that saw them he was dangerous. She could smell he was mated, but there was also other women's scents mixed along his skin, it took her a moment to realize it was Robin's scent. She knew Robin was mated, but she had never met him.

"It's okay, love, Adam Merks is my partner." Felix's hand ran up her back, soothing her before turning his attention back to Adam. "What's happening?"

Adam stopped in front of them, one hand in his pocket while his gun hand hung loose in case he had to go for his weapon. "The tigress that Pierce held captive, Daisy, she's freaking out. Ty has asked that we accompany him and Raja to make things clear to her. Robin, Tabitha, and Bethany are in the conference room already. If Harmony would like to join them, we can get this issue put to rest before the meeting. We're waiting for Connor to finish a search anyways."

Feeling the conflict in Felix, she looked at him. "Go. I don't need a babysitter. I told you I won't do anything stupid."

Ty stepped out of the conference room. "The women are waiting for her. I've left all the other guards with them."

"Stay with them." Felix looked directly into her eyes. "I'll be back as soon as I can." He walked her to the door, glancing around to see who was on guard.

"Stop worrying. Go do what you need to." She gave a gentle kiss to him before heading to join Robin, Tabitha and Bethany gathered around the table. She was eager to find out what changes Robin has experienced with the connection.

"Harmony," Robin called to her, nodding to the chair next to her. "Have you heard the news?"

"What news?" She strolled around the table and took the seat next to her. She felt Felix leave, his dread like a pit in her stomach. "Felix said there was a change with the connection—is that what you're talking about?"

"Yeah. We're still connected, and I feel you, actually stronger now that you're in the same room, but things are different. It's no longer as overpowering as what it was before. The connection is no longer tearing me apart. I'm not sure if you've slept yet, but if so, I no longer share your nightmares." The relief was clear as a tiger's claw cutting through skin.

"But how?" Harmony leaned back against the stiff leather of the chair, watching Robin closely. The dark shadows no longer hung under her eyes.

"Ty believes mating Felix has helped take the pressure from Robin, making things more bearable for her." Styx announced, coming to stand next to Shadow across from the women.

Harmony released a relieved sigh, happy that she was no longer screwing up Robin's life with her own turmoil. "Then I don't have to commit to Ty to make things easier for you. We don't have to worry about the issues that might cause."

"You're not going to commit to the clan even though you've mated with one of the Elder's guards?" Tabitha's voice held a note of surprise and concern.

Shit. How was she going to get out of this without sounding ungrateful? She should have watched her mouth around Tabitha, the Alpha Female and Ty's mate. "It's not that...I had a bad experience with my last Alpha. To commit myself to anyone might be asking too much of me."

"But you committed to Robin and to Felix. Through them you should be able to feel we are nothing like the one you had experience with." Tabitha eyed her with suspicion.

"I've thought about it, and I know it would make things easier for everyone involved, especially with my mating with Felix. I'm just not sure I can do it." Harmony ran her hand through her curls. "I'm torn. I don't want to be alone, but to commit myself to a clan and put myself back in the position I was in before is terrifying."

"So you just expect to live here with Felix, know our secrets, and yet not have any commitments to us?" Tabitha leaned forward, her gaze on Harmony.

"I didn't."

Tabitha held up her hand cutting Harmony off. "As Felix's mate you'd be entitled to attend the Elder meetings, know information concerning threats, upcoming missions, and more that I don't even want to think about at the moment. You'd be a security threat within the walls. We can't have that. I won't risk this clan."

Tabitha's words brought home the fact she was still in the same spot she was before. If she didn't commit to Ty and the clan, then she'd have issues. She wouldn't be able to help Connor with his search, and her computer hacker skills could come in handy for the clan. Was she willing to risk all to help them just because she was mated to Felix? Or was she content to sit on the sidelines and let them handle everything?

Trusting a Tiger: Alaskan Tigers

Chapter Eleven

Felix hated being separated from his mate, but this was his job. If Ty asked something of him, he'd do it. The clan meant everything to him, and mating didn't change that. Was he a better guard before his mating? How much was it going to reflect in him protecting Tabitha, and occasionally Ty?

When Adam first mated Robin, his attention was divided, part of that was because Robin was suffering from a panic attack from her time on the run from Pierce. As Robin began to trust Adam and the clan, he was able to return to his duties with no issues. Right now Felix could feel his attention divided between his duties to the clan and his need to be with his mate. He only prayed it was short term.

"What's the issue with Daisy?" Felix asked as he led Ty and Raja toward Daisy's cabin on the far side of the grounds. Adam brought up the rear, keeping the Elders between them. It didn't matter they were on the compound, they had implemented strong guidelines when guarding one of the Elders and their mates. The guards had to think of everyone as a threat to keep them safe.

"We found her father." There was a touch of hardness to Ty's voice, hinting to Felix that whatever news they were about to deliver to Daisy wasn't good.

Questions died on Felix's tongue as they stepped in front of Daisy's cabin. He raised his hand to knock on the door, barging in on her would only frighten her, not to mention how rude it would be. As a prisoner of Pierce for months, she had been through too much, including Pierce trying to produce an heir with her. They set Daisy up in one of the small guest cabins for privacy so she could adjust to her freedom.

The door swung open, and Daisy stood there glaring at them, completely covered by a turtleneck sweater and jeans, which hid her scars. Her red hair flowed around her while her gaze let them know she was not happy being disturbed. "What?" The lemony scent of her drifted to them, potent enough that Felix could almost taste it.

"May we come in?" Ty asked, stepping forward. As the Alpha of the clan, he had the right to enter any part of the compound without permission, but he gave her the illusion of an option to make her more at ease.

She stepped aside and allowed the four men to enter her small cabin. It was all one room but was spacious enough that it didn't feel cramped. The small kitchenette was just to the right of the doorway with the living area and bedroom space taking up the back portion. The television was on, but Felix knew from Adam's comments when they returned that she kept it on only for the noise because the silence reminded her of her captivity. Other than that, the only place in the cabin that looked lived-in was the bed. The blankets were twisted up, and Felix thought that was most likely from tossing and turning with nightmares.

As they entered, she scurried away, trying to keep as much distance between her and them. "I didn't do it—I haven't even left the cabin."

"We're not here because of anything you might have done. Why don't we have a seat?" Ty nodded toward the small living section.

Shaking her head 'no', she finally met Ty's gaze. "Please just tell me why you're here."

"We found your father." Ty leaned against the kitchenette counter. Raja stood next to him while Felix and Adam stood on each side, with Adam a little closer to the door to make sure no one else entered.

"My father." Relief flooded her voice, and her shoulders relaxed. This was her way out of Alaska and away from other tigers. She didn't trust anyone, and being here surrounded by people was more than she wanted. Instead she hid away in the cabin, seeing no one. "Where is he? Is he okay?"

Ty took a step forward, but she backed away. "I'm sorry."

"No! It can't be." Her legs struggled to hold her before finally giving away, and she collapsed onto the floor.

Felix watched her with interest. She looked so much like his mate, the same fiery red hair, the broken spirit. The resemblance was uncanny. He couldn't help thinking that they could have been sisters, but he knew that Harmony's parents died long ago, leaving her alone.

As far as she knew, there was no other family, except him now that they were mated.

"Connor found the records this morning. He was killed nearly six months ago." Ty's voice was soft and full of compassion. From years of working with Ty, Felix had learned this was one of the duties of the Alpha that Ty detested.

"How?" Tears welled in her eyes, but none fell. Daisy held her emotions close to the vest. It's what kept her alive with Pierce and what helped her from losing her mind during the days locked in a small crawl space, waiting for Pierce to decide it was time to use or torture her.

Ty shook his head. "You don't need the details."

"Pierce said he went looking for me at my father's. He said he didn't harm him. Why?"

Felix wasn't surprised that Pierce lied to her—after all, he was a rogue. One that killed many times before Ty, Adam, and the rest of the team eliminated him. "Why was he looking for you?"

"His partner Victor did some work with my father. One time, not long after Dad and I left the clan for his work, Victor was visiting—something to do with the project Dad was working on. Pierce came with him. We didn't know it was Pierce then or Dad would have contacted you. We knew you were hunting him. Victor introduced him as J.J."

J.J.? As in Bethany's rogue cousin who transformed Pierce into a rogue? Felix looked at Ty, who shook his head. This was not something that should be mentioned in front of an outsider, but Ty caught the same thing.

Squeezing her eyes shut, she took a deep breath. "Did Pierce kill him?"

"What we found leads us to believe he did." Ty nodded. "You're welcome to stay here as long as you wish or to move on to another clan if you wish."

"Thank you."

With nothing more to say, they moved to the door, leaving Daisy alone with her grief. When they were far enough away from Daisy's cabin, they stopped for a chance to touch base on what just happened without anyone overhearing them before they made it back to the conference room.

"Why would he pretend to be J.J.?" Adam looked at Ty as if hoping he had the answer.

Ty shook his head, sending his shoulder-length hair flying in the wind. "I don't know, but we'll find out. He wouldn't have wanted to tell him his name because he had to realize they would know who he was—but to say he was J.J. seems unusual even for him."

Felix's brain was working overtime trying to come up with something that made sense. "When J.J. transformed him, do you think a part of him transferred to Pierce?"

Ty raised a questioning eyebrow at him. "Why would you ask that?"

"I can't explain it, but I think Daisy and Harmony are related. Besides the fact they look so much alike, there's something about

Daisy that reminds me of my mate. Harmony met Bethany's Uncle James and J.J. years ago when J.J. was only a boy. Maybe part of that stayed with him. If a portion of J.J. transferred over to Pierce with the bite, it would explain why Pierce had such interest in Daisy, because she reminded him of someone from the past," Felix explained, hoping that it was making sense because his thoughts were all over the place on it. To him it seemed logical but explaining it was more difficult then he thought.

"It's possible. After the conference, I'll speak with Doc to see if he thinks it could happen. For a shifter to bite someone is rare, so we have very little data on actual weres." Ty tugged his hair back into a leather strap to keep it out of his face.

"Are you sure they're related?" Raja inquired.

Knowing what he recognized, he nodded. "Doc could do a DNA test, but I feel something there. It feels like a family connection, but not one they recognize yet."

"Very well. Find out if Harmony has any idea if she's related to Daisy. We'll have Doc do the DNA test if she doesn't." Ty shoved his hands into the pockets of his jeans. "Let's get back to the women and make some decisions on Henry."

Felix turned to continue back to the conference room, and his thoughts turned back to Harmony. How would she feel about a possible cousin? Daisy was a security threat to the clan with no loyalties to anyone. He couldn't trust his mate alone with her, even if they were related.

He opened the door, checking the hallway before allowing the Elders to step in with Adam behind them. Commotion from the end of the conference room caught his attention. *What the hell is going on now?* He sped up his pace, knowing the others would do the same. He didn't bother to order Adam to keep the Elders away—their mates were there, and all of them would risk their lives for the women.

"Milo, please escort Harmony to the cafeteria. You two can have coffee or something, and Felix will come and get you when this is over," Tabitha ordered just as Felix stepped into the room.

"What's going on? Ty said Harmony could attend the Elder meetings once we were mated."

Tabitha shook her head. "She's a security threat."

"What?" Felix moved further into the room until he was standing next to his mate.

"While we were talking, she said she would not be committing to the clan. With no commitment, she has no loyalty to us. I won't risk the clan." Tabitha turned to her mate looking for support on the matter. "You even said she couldn't help Connor without the commitment. Same goes for the meetings. There's too much sensitive material covered in one of the Elder meetings. Without her loyalty, there's no guarantee she won't betray us."

Coming to stand by his mate, Ty nodded. "I believed that once the two of you were mated, Harmony would be willing to commit to the clan. Now that the bond between Robin and Harmony has lessened with the mating, there's no guarantee that Robin would be aware if there was a chance she'd betray the clan. I'm sorry, Felix, but you're too involved emotionally and mentally with her. You could overlook something because you don't want to believe that your mate would risk your clan. Tabitha's right—without the commitment to the clan, Harmony's a security threat."

"I can't believe you'll stand there and deny my mate after everything I've done for this clan!" Felix was shocked by what he was hearing.

"Allowing your mate into the private details would risk *my* mate, and I won't do that for someone who's denying a clan that opened its arms and doors to her." Ty's eyes showed the fire of his temper, but his words were calm.

Felix stared across the room at Ty. His beast wanted to stand up for his mate—to scream at Ty. The rational part of him knew Ty was right. They couldn't risk the clan no matter whose mate she was. It was too dangerous for the Alaskan Tigers now, but even thinking logically, he couldn't suppress his beast's anger.

Harmony laid a hand on his cheek, forcing him to look away from Ty. "It's okay. I don't want to be somewhere I'm not welcomed."

Before he could stifle it, a growl tore through his throat. His beast provoked him to challenge his Alpha, and he pushed Harmony aside and stepped towards Ty.

Raja stepped in front of Ty. As the clan's Lieutenant one of his jobs was to protect the Alpha, and he stood there, blocking direct access to Ty. "Don't do something you'll regret, Felix."

It was enough for Felix to rein-in his tiger. He didn't want to go up against his Alpha. Ty and Tabitha were the ones that would bring peace to their kind, and fighting amongst themselves wouldn't help things. This was put into motion because of Harmony's choice. Even with the mating, she didn't truly trust him or what she was feeling. He'd have to find another way to prove himself and the clan to her.

"You can join her if you wish, and we'll have this meeting without you." Ty pulled Felix's attention back to him. Even surrounded by Raja, Adam and Styx, there was no doubt to anyone in the room that Ty was in charge. He'd fight his own fight if it came to that with Felix.

"Don't, Felix." Harmony came back up to him. "This isn't worth it. When I accepted the mating, I knew who you were and your position. Your clan needs you now." She reached out for him, taking his hand in hers and giving it a squeeze. "Find me when you're done. You know where I'll be." With that, she stepped away from him.

"Don't leave the grounds," he called after her as she strolled through the door.

"Shall I go with her?" Milo questioned from his spot by Bethany where he watched things play out.

"She'll be fine." Felix growled, angry with himself, Harmony, and the whole situation. "Let's get this over with so I can get back to my mate."

"You're angry about it now, but you know it's the right decision. Things are too dangerous to take any risks." Tabitha slid her arm around Ty again now that things had calmed.

"I know, and that makes it harder. Damn it! Why can't she just make things easier?" Felix pulled out one of the leather conference chairs and sank down on it, his shoulders sagging slightly in defeat.

Ty's joyous laughter filled the room. "Mating is never easy. You're fooling yourself if you think you're going to have it easy."

"I'm finding that out. She's accepted me as her mate because she has no choice—the mating desire caused her enough pain that she gave in—but every time she looks at me, she sees Henry." Felix used his forefinger and thumb to rub his eyes. "What are we going to do about Henry?"

"Eliminate him?" When all eyes turned to Adam, he added. "What choice do we have?"

"You're right, we don't have a choice, but what I meant is, are we going to wait for him to come after Harmony or are we going after him?" Felix smiled at the fact his partner was so outspoken. He was willing to state what needed to be done, even if he encountered Felix's wrath later. If only he could have been that forward years ago when Henry and he came into their beast...maybe they wouldn't be in this situation now.

"We know he landed in Seattle, but do we know anything else?" Styx spoke up for the first time.

"When Felix was on the phone with Ty, news came in that Henry booked a car. We suspected it was to drive to Fairbanks. But since then, he also booked a seat on the only flight from Seattle to Fairbanks today. It leaves in less than an hour, but we're not sure which way he's coming."

Connor sat at the table looking as though he had been raised with the clan. No one would have realized that Connor, the clan's geek, was a wolf shifter until they smelled the musky, woody smell that was entirely Connor. "With so many searches, Lukas and I are working around the clock, but we don't have any new information on Henry at this time. He hasn't returned the car yet, or at least it hasn't been updated in their system. Depending on if he used the key drop or clerk, it could take a little time. As far as we know, he's in Seattle still. He hasn't checked in for the flight yet."

"It's possible he doesn't know Harmony didn't make it to Seattle." Felix had kept his mate occupied during the night so she didn't have time for anything else. "Now with our mating, it's broken the connection Henry had with her, so she can no longer give him the message. But he'll figured it out and come after her unless we get to him first."

"Does she still have her cell phone? He might call it, and I have the tracer activated on it." Connor tried to stifle a yawn.

Felix nodded, knowing where he was going with the questions. "She has it, but it's off. I can have her turn it back on when we're done here. It's worth a try."

"Connor, you're exhausted," Robin chimed in. "Why don't you get some sleep, and I'll help Lukas go through the scans for a few hours. When you get up, then he can get some sleep. You can't keep going on like this." Robin was always concerned with everyone else. She was the caregiver of the Elder team.

"Thanks, when we're done here." He yawned again before turning to Felix. "If you can convince your mate to commit to the clan, I could sure use her help. She must have some mad skills just from what Robin's learned from her connection to Harmony."

"I'll see what I can do. I know she considers herself a hacker, which is how she made enough to support herself outside of the Ohio land." His mate would be a good addition to the clan's nerd crew if he could just get her to see that they were different than her Ohio clan.

"If he made it to Fairbanks, do you think you'd be able to feel him?" Raja steered the meeting back on track.

"He'd be close enough that I would hope so, but like I said, the sibling connection has never been strong since Henry doesn't shift." He rested his head against the back of the chair. "As much as I want this over, until we know where Henry is, we can't go off after him. We don't know for certain he's still in Seattle, so I don't think we should go after him. He could be on his way here, and we could miss him."

"Agreed. Go to your mate, turn the cell phone on, and we'll see if he contacts her. With luck Connor can pinpoint Henry's location and we can take him down before gets near the compound. Until then we need to be on alert and ready at a moment's notice. In the meantime, see if you can make progress with her," Ty ordered.

Everyone rose, ready to get back to what they were doing before the meeting. Felix stood, stretching out his long legs. He was eager to find Harmony to see what damage being denied into the meetings had done to the progress he had made with her.

"Wait a moment, Felix," Ty hollered to him before he could get to the door.

He paused, the tension tightened his muscles as he waited for Ty to knock him back to his place after his display before the meeting. When nothing came, he asked. "Everything okay?"

"Come with me." Ty led Felix away from the group, causing the anxiety to rise further. Down the hall, out of hearing range of the others still gathered in the conference room, he stopped. "I've been giving this a great deal of thought, and I know what I'm about to tell you won't make you happy but it needs to be said. You've been an important part of this clan—and I don't want that to change—but Harmony isn't going to make things easy. Without her commitment, I can't have her in the main building. She's too much of a risk."

"What? It's one thing not having her in the Elder meetings, but this is uncalled for!"

"Not when it comes to protecting the mates and clan. There's too much of a chance she could hear something, and even with guards, the mates are here. I won't risk Tabby and Bethany to save face with your stubborn mate." Ty crossed his arms over his broad chest. "If you wish to take a leave from your duties for a bit, I can make arrangements. With Tad, Theodore and Carran, there are enough guards to keep Tabitha safe, and Adam can take over your other duties."

Felix had to bite his tongue. He wanted to tell Ty to shove the job up his ass, as if he didn't care, but no matter what Ty said, he couldn't do that. He had worked too hard for his position in the clan, and he wouldn't give that up, not even for his mate. Somehow, he'd find a way to divide his attentions to keep things equal without slacking on his duties to the clan. "No, I made my commitment to this clan and Tabitha long before the uphill battle of mating started. I'll convince her to commit to the clan."

"It needs to be her decision. If you force it, she'll regret it, and it will cause tension between you two. It's possible that once we eliminate Henry it will help, especially now that the Ohio Alpha is no longer a threat."

"Eliminating Henry could take years. Look how long we were after Pierce before you were able to take him down. Still now there are others who have taken his place. The threats to the clan and the mates won't end until there's peace for our kind. For that to happen, I need to find a way to do my duties and deal with a mate that is uncooperative." Felix didn't have the patience to wait years for Henry to no longer be a threat to Harmony and the clan, even if that meant he had to go after him alone.

Chapter Twelve

Tossing rocks at the creek, Harmony tried to let her anger go. She hated being kept in the dark about things that concerned her. Henry was coming after her, not the clan, and keeping information from her when it was her safety at risk was unacceptable. How was she supposed to believe they were so different from the Ohio Alpha after this? "Damn it, why did I let Felix drag me back?"

"Because the mating desire had taken hold," Felix reminded her as he stepped out from the trees coming toward her.

Her breath caught in her throat from fear. She let her guard down, lost in the reel of emotions and didn't even sense him coming. Mates rarely were able to sneak up on each other because they were so in tune with each other, but she was too emotional to be focused.

Seeing him sneak up on her from behind the trees reminded her once again how closely he resembled Henry, at least at a distance. When they were close, she could see the subtle changes, run her fingers over the deep dimples, and his personality never let her forget they were different. It was just from a distance that it sent fear coursing through her again.

"You're done?" Even as the words left her mouth, she knew it was stupid—if he wasn't done, then he wouldn't be standing in front of her.

"For now." He closed the last remaining distance and sat down next to her, holding her cell phone out to her. "Here, I've turned this back on to see if Henry calls you. We need to pinpoint his location, and if you can keep him on the phone for at least sixty seconds, Connor will be able to trace it."

"I don't want to talk to him." It might have been childish, but it was the truth, every time she thought about him, she had to fight the distance it was causing between her and Felix. Speaking to him and hearing the threats from a voice that was too close to Felix's for her taste would only make it harder to fight.

"If we want to find him before he makes it to the compound, it's our best option. If you'd prefer to wait until he arrives here, then I'll respect your decision. It will put you and the others at more risk, but I won't force you to do this if you're against it."

His words sent the guilt rushing through her. Keeping the others safe was the reason she fled the compound in the first place. Now he sat there using her reasoning against her. *Damn him.* "Fine, I'll do it." She snatched the phone from his hand.

They sat there in silence for a while, watching the salmon swim down the creek. It was one of the added features for Kallie's mates and the rest of the Kodiak Bears that would visit occasionally. Felix finally turned to her and broached the subject she knew had been hanging in the balance since she left the conference room. "We're going to have to discuss your unwillingness to commit to the clan."

"What do you want me to say?" She leaned back against the tree, refusing to meet his gaze. "Are you or Ty going to force the commitment?"

"No, it needs to be done of your own free will. But you need to realize how hard this will make it on our mating."

Hidden words lay within that statement, because she could feel his concern on what it would do to his career. He had worked long and hard to gain the position and respect of the clan and to have a mate not committed to something that was his heart and soul would look bad for him. It could also cause tension and problems with the Elders and clan members. "Couldn't we just focus on Henry for now?"

"Fine." He stretched his legs out in front of him and continued to gaze at the creek. "Let's discuss your family then. You mentioned your parents died when you were young, leaving you the cottage near your clan's land where you stayed by yourself. Did they have any siblings? Cousins?"

"Mom had a sister, but I never met her. She died from complications during childbirth. The father raised the child, but that's all I know. It's the only family that I have, and I've never even met my cousin and her father. Why?"

"When the team took down Pierce, they found a prisoner. I believe she's your cousin." Felix turned to lie on his side to watch her.

"What?"

"She has the same ruby red hair and other features that peaked my interest, which is when I sensed the family connection. I think when you met J.J. that you made an impression on him. It transferred to Pierce when he was bit by J.J., and that's why he kept Daisy prisoner. Doc can do a DNA test to be sure, but it would explain things."

Daisy? She tried to think back—way back to when she was a child, trying to remember if her mother ever mentioned the girl's name. Nothing solid came to mind, but the name Daisy rang a bell in her head.

"Did you ask her?" She couldn't wrap her mind around the fact that she might have family.

"Not yet. It wasn't until after we left that I was able to put the pieces together, and I wanted to speak with you first. She spent too long under Pierce's control, and as you were when you came here, she is untrusting. Daisy grew up among the clan as a child before her father's job took her out of the country, so she's coming around quicker than expected. I'm not sure she's up for company, but she might welcome a family member, especially since you've had similar experiences. You might be able to provide comfort for one another."

"I'm not ready to see her. Have Doc do the DNA test first. I don't want to get my hopes up that I have a cousin if in reality we just have the same hair color. Red hair is uncommon but not unheard of." She reached out to him, cupping his cheek. "Instead of talking about everyone else, how about we focus on us before something else comes up to draw you away from me."

"What exactly do you have in mind?" He scooted toward her, bringing their faces close together.

"I think you know what I have in mind." She breathed him in, enjoying the spicy aroma so manly and full of life. "I want you, Felix."

"I figured after what happened earlier, that you'd want distance."

"Enough talk." She pressed her lips to his, tasting the coffee and vanilla creamer he favored still on his lips. The blood heated as it rushed through her veins, warming her with desire. Sliding her tongue between his lips, she explored the contours of his mouth, drinking him in. "I want you now. Take me here…make this place special to us."

"Here? Someone could stumble upon us."

"Is my fierce tiger shy?" She teased, working his shirt from the waistband of his jeans. "Don't make me wait."

"I live to please you." His fingers unhooked the button of her jeans before slowing sliding down the zipper and tugging them off her with one quick motion. With her naked from the waist down, he slid his finger between her legs to the center of her body.

His fingers teased the sensitive numb before sliding a finger inside her core, stealing all logical thought. She fumbled with his belt, no longer able to handle the simple task as her desire began to overtake her. Closing her eyes, she enjoyed the sensations, while he planted sweet kisses along the curve of her neck. She wanted him more than she wanted her next breath.

With a nip to her neck, he moved down her body with his eyes locked on hers. His fingers working her into a state of frenzy. With every touch and tease, her body demanded more of him. Nudging her legs further apart, he slid between them, cupping her hips and kissing along her thighs before replacing his hand with his mouth. Tiny nips and gentle licks flicked over her sweet spot, nearly propelling her over the edge. Digging her nails into his back, she cried out for him as her ecstasy neared. "Felix!"

With one last flick of the tongue, he pulled away from her. "Not yet mate. I want to be inside you first."

Using his shirt, she pulled him back up the length of her body. "What are you waiting for?"

"You're so demanding, love." Rising to his knees between her body, he finished loosening his jeans, freeing his erection.

Reaching out, she wrapped her hand around his shaft, feeling the hardness of it. His pulse beat through it and into her hand. Teasing her hand along the length of it until she reached the tip, she leaned closer wanting to take him in her mouth to taste pre-cum and desire for her.

"No, I won't last."

"Just a little. I want to feel you in my mouth." She pushed forward, drawing her tongue along the tip. His fingers dug into her hair, as she slid her mouth around him. Her throat tensed with the gag reflex, almost forcing him out of her mouth. She waited, tasting the saltiness of him and letting herself get used to the feel of him before working her mouth up and down the length of him. He was too long to fit completely in her mouth, so to make up for it, she wrapped her hand around the base and slid her hand up and down the rest of his shaft as she worked her mouth around him.

Playful she dragged her tongue along the length of him before taking him back into her mouth. He arched into her, sliding deeper in her mouth, his hand still deep in her hair, making it impossible for her to move away unless she was willing loss hair.

He pulled back, vacating her mouth and leaving her feel empty. "Stand up."

She stood, careful to avoid any sharp rocks or branches with her bare feet. Before she could question why he wanted her to stand, he lifted her against his chest and pushed her against the tree she had been leaning against before. Gently he lowered her, sliding her onto his shaft until he filled her completely.

"Wrap your legs around me but not too tight." The tension in him made his voice deep and raspy.

She did as he asked and also wrapped her arms around his neck, bringing her lips to hover just above his. "I need you," she begged.

He gripped her hips and used the space between them to slide almost completely out of her before slamming home again. His manhood filled her completely, and with each stroke the tempo intensified another level as they found the rhythm they needed to keep their balance. Their hips slammed together, driving her closer and closer to her release. She dug her nails into his back. Their thrusts grew deeper and faster, moving with the precision of lovers who knew the special places of their mate. Their bodies rocked back and forth, tension stretching her tight as she fought for her release.

She arched her body into his, and screamed his name as her release coursed through her. He pumped twice more and growled her name as he released his seed into her.

She went limp in his embrace, resting her head in the nook of his shoulder as she tried to find the breath she had lost. Her heart was beating with such intensity she thought it would fly out of her chest. "Oh, Felix," she whispered as he squeezed her tightly against him.

"Harmony, never doubt I love you."

The way he said it made her fear that things were coming that would tear them apart, but she chose to hold onto that moment. She was going to enjoy the embrace of her mate until the next issue rose to bite her in the ass. "I love you, too," she whispered, still struggling to regain her breath.

Chapter Thirteen

Dusk was falling around the compound when they finally made it back from the creek. Harmony's legs were weak, and her body was exhausted. If it wasn't for Felix's arm around her waist, she wasn't sure she wouldn't have had the strength to make it back. All she wanted to do was crawl into bed and forget about the day. She had some major decisions to make, the biggest one being what she wanted to do about the clan. Was she willing to commit herself and once again be under an Alpha that held her life in his hands? Could she trust that Ty wouldn't trade her to further the clan's agenda?

Not committing to the clan would cause tension not only between Felix and her but also between him and the clan. Her happiness hinged on finding a way to balance the clan and her sanity.

"Harmony," Robin called to her as they stepped out of the trees.

Felix must have felt her body tense at the presence of the man with Robin, because he ran his fingers down her side, teasing along her hipbone. "That's Tex. He's new to the clan. No sudden movements—he's still a little spookable."

Robin and Tex closed the distance, meeting them halfway. The dark circles that were under Robin's eyes days before were fading, and for the first time since Harmony arrived, she seemed to be at peace. The dimming of the connection between them once Harmony mated seemed to have helped ease the tension in Robin.

"We were just about to grab some coffee. Would you like to join us?" Robin asked nodding to Tex.

"Umm." Harmony didn't want to but couldn't think of a polite way to bow out.

"Come on. I got hung up at the meeting but wanted to talk with you."

"Go ahead," Felix urged. "I need to check in on some stuff, and then I'll meet you back at your place in a bit."

She took a deep breath and tried not to give in to her irritation that the clan was once again coming between her and her mate. Resentment would only make things that much more strained. Trying to cherish each moment with him that she had, she let it go and turned back to Robin. "Okay," she nodded.

"Tex is new to the clan as well. He's from Texas," Robin explained leading them toward the cafeteria.

With a raised eyebrow, she took in the man next to her. He was the average cowboy, his tight jeans, black cowboy boots, and white cowboy hat firmly in place. "Texas? Wow, what brought you to Alaska?"

"Robin…"

"Go ahead." Robin nodded, leaving Harmony confused.

"When Adam went to rescue Robin in Texas, I was wounded by a rogue, and they had no choice but to bring me back with them to their healers. Long story short, I couldn't go back to my clan. Avery was using the clan members in ways no Alpha ever should." Holding open the door, he allowed her to enter the building before continuing. "I arrived about the same time you did, and it's been the best thing in my life. The Alaskan Tigers have given me a new start in life, and it can give you the same if you're willing to embrace it."

"Embrace it? You mean commit myself to the clan?" Harmony couldn't keep the surprise out of her voice. Did Robin or Felix encourage him to approach the subject with her? Adding more pressure to her wouldn't help her make the decision…if anything, it might hinder her more. She didn't want to be pressured.

He paused, glancing toward her as if truly taking her in. "If that's what you'd like, that decision has to be your own. I wasn't aware you weren't committed. I only mentioned it because I'm aware of the threat against you. I have faith that the clan will eliminate Henry and keep you safe."

"I hope so." If they didn't, it wasn't just her life on the line.

"Let's not talk about any of that," Robin said wearily, "We're supposed to be having a friendly coffee break. We're not to discuss the shit of the past, the uncertain future, and most certainly not the threats that are hanging over our heads."

Tex tipped his head toward Robin. "Ignore her. She's just exhausted after hearing of my past. She's hoping for something stronger than just coffee after hearing what Avery did to those under him."

Robin let out a deep sigh. "Since mating with Adam, I've been working on finishing my last psychology class for my license but have already started providing counseling to the clan and shifters in need. There was no one to help shifters through things in the past—they couldn't go to a human without exposing us—now I'm helping to fill that role."

"That's great, Robin. It's something we don't have, but I know we could use. Maybe you can get others to consider that profession for other clans. I know some Alphas have paid to put a clan member through school to be a doctor or lawyer, giving the clan the professional experience with the shifter knowledge." Maybe if she had someone to speak with all those years ago, she wouldn't have let things get so bad with her former Alpha.

The sweet, heavenly aroma of rich coffee filled the room as they poured it into their mugs. Each made their coffee to their tastes, Harmony adding a splash of vanilla creamer until it was a warm brown. At this time of day, the cafeteria was empty, giving them their choice of seats as they moved away from the coffee bar.

They slid into one of the round booths, giving them a view of the room. "It will only work in some clans, but I do hope I can help make changes in the shifter world where psychology is concerned. Shifters need someone they can talk to just as much as humans, and there's nothing wrong with that."

"What do you mean 'only in some clans'?" Harmony took the seat next to Robin as Tex took the other side, placing Robin in the middle of the booth.

"It will only work if the shifter in question who has sought help can receive it without the Alpha demanding to know everything. A counselor would have to report to the Alpha if they felt the patient or someone else's life was in jeopardy, but other secrets would be kept between the counselor and client or there would never be any progress." Robin looked to Tex before taking a sip of her coffee.

"She's right. Even if she had been in Texas, I could have never gone to her. Patient's privacy was never part of Avery's language. No matter what was said or to whom, Avery wanted to know. I was doomed to suffer silently under Avery's hand until Robin and Adam came along." He laid his hand over Robin's arm. "I'll never be able to repay you for picking Royalwood to hide out. If I hadn't been at the airstrip guarding Adam's helicopter against Pierce's rogues, I'd have still been left to that fate. I have no doubt that in the end he'd have killed me."

Robin smiled, the bond between them unmistakable. "To have to suffer one day under the hands of an abusive or controlling Alpha is too much, but to think of a lifetime under one is unspeakable. I'll do what I can do make the shifter world a better one."

"Unfortunately," Harmony replied, "you don't know the Alpha's true ways until it's too late and you've committed yourself to the clan." She flipped her hair over her shoulder out of her way before bringing the hot cup of coffee to her lips.

"You're thinking Ty's hiding his true nature from you?" Robin asked incredulously. "Then explain why you feel the loyalty that Felix has to Ty and the clan? Why no matter who you ask in the clan they don't have a negative word to say about him? Why would Jinx and the West Virginia Tigers—or Taber, Thorben and the rest of the Kodiak Bears—follow Ty's lead? Surely another Alpha would recognize if Ty were hiding something and wouldn't follow him blindly. Everyone couldn't be in on the conspiracy to hide Ty's 'true nature' from you." Robin's words were harsh but added some perceptive to the situation.

Tex leaned forward, resting his elbows on the table. His hands were wrapped around the coffee mug in front of him, watching Harmony as if trying to understand her logic. "If Ty was as you think he is, he wouldn't care that Avery is abusing his people, but he does. He's working to do something about it. The clan was after Pierce for years trying to take him down, and they continued the search even when Pierce left them alone. Ty is trying to make it a safe world not only for tigers but for all shifters."

"It all sounds logical enough and I feel Felix's commitment to the clan, but I can't put my past experiences out of my mind. Robin, I don't expect you to understand. You're human and never had to deal with this until you mated, so you don't fully understand what some shifters are like. But you, Tex—I would expect you to understand. How can you commit yourself to Ty when you've spent years under Avery?"

"Robin and the other clan members helped me see the light. The Elders were willing to take me in and stand up against Avery to protect me. Even now they are still fighting for me, since I hold too many of his secrets for Avery to let me go without a fight." Tex's gaze narrowed down at her, letting her know that he believe she was being naïve.

"I might have never had any experiences with shifters or Alphas before, but it's not hard to comprehend. More importantly, I've seen Ty's and the Elders' commitment to the clan and to keeping shifters as a whole safe. I'm tired of defending the people I care about to you. You may doubt them, but I've had enough of it. When you're ready to open your eyes to the opportunity you have before you then let me know. Otherwise, I'm done." Robin rose, taking her coffee with her as she did, and left Harmony staring after her.

"It would seem that you've pissed Robin off." Tex took a long drink of his coffee. "I've never seen her lose her patience."

"She just doesn't understand." She pushed her coffee off to the side, no longer interested in it.

He drained his coffee before meeting her gaze. "No, Harmony, I think it's you that doesn't understand." He pushed back from the table and stood. "I have to say: I agree with Robin. You're mated to one of the top Elder guards, which means you have certain responsibilities."

Tex left her, leaving her alone with her thoughts. To say she was shocked by the outcome would be an understatement. She sat there unable to believe that everyone was against her. Was she really on the wrong side of things? Was she letting her prejudices of her previous Alpha get in the way of what was happening here? Maybe she was, but she wasn't sure how to move past it.

* * *

Felix entered the world of the geeks seeking Connor and the newest information on the clan's missions, especially Henry. In the hours he spent making love to Harmony by the creek, did Henry make his way to them? Did he travel by plane or car? If by plane, he would already be here, but by car they had another few hours before he'd be close enough to be an immediate threat.

Computers were set up at a number of stations throughout the room, most of them having more than one computer monitor hooked up to make multitasking easier. A small coffee station sat in the corner, looking well-used with a number of mugs and energy drinks scattered throughout. Connor and Lukas were the main geeks of the compound, but sometimes Robin or the Elders would assist.

Connor looked up from the laptop in front of him. "Hey, Felix, I thought you'd be off using your ways of persuasion to convince your mate to join the clan. I could use her skills in here."

"I'm doing what I can, but it seems my tigress is hardheaded." He strolled across the room until he came to Connor's area where he plopped down in the chair beside the desk. "Update me. What have you found since the meeting? Henry's status?"

"He took the plane, which landed an hour ago, and picked up a rental car fifteen minutes ago. I just alerted Ty of this. I believe he's planning to put a team together to try to intercept him before he makes it this far. He was going to contact you once things were gearing up, figuring you'd want to be a part of the team." Connor grabbed the coffee from the table and leaned back. "Avery's threatening to go to war over Tex. We've got to take care of the situation with Henry so we can deal with the Texas clan. We're too small of a clan to be divided up on missions."

For a wolf shifter, Connor was greatly in tune with the needs of the clan. The Alaskan Tigers had opened their home and hearts to him, giving him a safe haven after his narrow escape from Pierce's control. He had proven himself loyal to the clan time and time again, always going above and beyond the call of duty.

"I'll get with Ty. With luck on our side, we'll take Henry out of the equation by this time tomorrow and can focus on Avery. I noticed that Tex has adjusted well to the clan. He'll be a great addition to the fight." With new determination, Felix rose to find Ty. "Don't forget Randolph and the rogues Pierce left behind. Once they get their legs under them again, it's possible they'll cause havoc for us."

"I'm aware and have been keeping an eye on their activities as best I can."

In search of Ty, Felix strolled out the door with his thoughts turning back to his mate. How difficult would things be in his clan if she refused to commit herself to Ty? It would obviously mean there would be much tension and many secrets between him and his mate, because he wouldn't be able to share any details of the clan's activities with her until it was public knowledge for the whole clan. Not to mention the issue of living arrangements. He couldn't stay in her apartment because it was too far from his duties, and she couldn't join him in the main building. There was no way she'd be allowed to his quarters once the second floor was complete, making matters even worse. Mating was supposed to be the happiest time in a shifters life. Instead, for Felix, it was turning out to confusing and problematic.

"Felix, I was just coming to find you." Ty's voice traveled down the hall toward Felix, pulling him from his thoughts with a jerk.

"Harmony's having coffee with Robin and Tex, so I was catching up on things. I stopped by and talked to Connor. He brought me up to speed. When are we heading out? If you haven't appointed someone else, I'd like to command the team."

"You were our first choice. Taber and Styx are standing by. If there are others you'd like, get them ready. Adam has asked to accompany you as well."

Felix cocked his head to the side. "Is that wise? I wouldn't want to take Tabitha's best guards from her. I hope the mission will be a success without any outfall, but as you're aware, things can go wrong. Adam should stay to keep Tabitha safe in case…" The words *something should happen* died on his tongue. He knew the risks—they all did—but that didn't keep them in the safety of the compound waiting for trouble to find them.

"That 'in case' is exactly why Adam should go with you. The two of you are an excellent team. To have him protecting your back will ensure you both come back safely. Besides, Carran has been proving himself under Adam and Tad, so Tabby will still have three guards while you and Adam are gone. Theodore will be arriving within the hour. After the latest threat from Avery, we wanted any extra hands on board we could get. Jinx is standing by, along with a few members of his clan if we need them as well. If I feel the threat has increased, there are always Bethany's guards. We'll keep the women together if we have to. We'll make it work. Adam needs to go." Ty hooked his thumbs through his belt loops and watched Felix.

"'Needs to go'… as in another of Tabitha's messages from the book?" He was well aware of the book that had guided Tabitha along the path so far and would continue to do so, helping her unite the tiger shifters. If the book told Tabitha that Adam needed to go, then no one would argue. You didn't go against the book if you wanted to survive whatever threat they were facing.

Ty nodded. "I'm sending Galen as well. You have fifteen minutes until the team is ready. I've sent them to gear up, if you're going be out in front of the main compound then."

"I'll be there. I need to tell Harmony something." He took a quick look at his cell phone, checking the time.

Ty's jaw tightened with unsaid words. His body was ridged, screaming just how displeased he was about the situation involving Harmony. "Let her know you're going after Henry, but that's all. I'm going to have her guarded until you return. I don't want any unfortunate incidents like before. Without the connection between her and the clan and with the bond between her and Robin dimmed from your mating, I can't risk her leaving the compound. Jayden will take the first watch., I'll send him to find her shortly. Go to your mate. Hopefully when this is over, we can put this behind us, and she can do what needs to be done."

"Yes, sir." Felix spun around, heading directly to his room. Going after Henry, Felix needed more than just the firearm in his shoulder holster. He wanted to be fully loaded. Taking no chances when it came to Henry would bring him and his team home. Brother, you brought this upon yourself.

Chapter Fourteen

Long after the others had left, Harmony sat there. At some point, Harmony had wrapped her hands around her mug of coffee, giving her something to hold onto. The coffee inside had grown cold, not that she had any desire to drink it now. She tried not to think, just to be there unattached. Thinking would only lead her to the conclusion that Robin and Tex were right. *Damn it!*

"There you are," Felix called as he strode toward her.

Her gaze met his, taking him in. His jeans and T-shirt were now replaced with black cargo pants and a black long-sleeve shirt. Completing the outfit was a bulletproof vest pulled tight over his broad chest. No longer did he wear his shoulder holster, instead there was an assault rifle slung over his chest and an additional handgun in a thigh holster and a knife on his belt.

"What's happening?" She pushed the coffee away and rose.

"I only have a few minutes, but I wanted you to know I'm going after Henry." He closed the distance and wrapped his arms around her, pulling her into his body.

"No, you can't. Let someone else." The rough material of his bulletproof vest against her body brought home the direness of the situation.

"I can't. He's my brother, which makes it my responsibility. I'll be back." His hands caressed her back, and he buried his face in her hair.

There was that word 'responsibilities' again, reminding her she now had them as well. Why were things so difficult when all she really wanted was for things to be simple? She wanted an uncomplicated life with her mate. "You'd choose finding Henry over me?" Even as the words left her mouth, she knew they were selfish and stupid.

His body went stiff under her touch. "I'm not doing that. I'm going after him to protect you and to protect this clan and other shifters and humans."

"Go then!" She pulled away from him, taking a step back.

"Harmony…"

"Just go." She continued to step back away from him, doing her best to distance herself from him physically and emotionally. The hurt and anger was clear on his face, but she couldn't let herself go to him, knowing there was a real possibility he wouldn't be returning to her. If Henry killed him, she'd be forced from the clan unless she was willing to commit to them, leaving her alone in the world again. She wasn't sure she could handle that.

"No, I won't just go. Damn it, Harmony, I'm doing this for you—for us. Don't be so callous that you can't see that. If he's eliminated, maybe you can put your past behind you."

"Why? So I commit to your clan? Is that the reason behind all of this?" Anger heated her words.

He closed the distance she put between them in a blink of an eye, wrapping his hands around her arms. Her body stiffened under his grip, and anger vibrated through him. "Shit, woman, how can you even think that? Maybe when this is done, you can look at me and see me, not Henry. Every time you look at me, I can see you waiting for me to hurt you, to do the things he did to you. My words won't change your mind that I'm not him, but maybe this will. Maybe you will finally be able to put Henry to rest—to accept our mating without wondering when I'll do something that he did to you."

Heavy soled boots thumped as someone entered the cafeteria. "Felix, you're needed."

With one last look, he let his hands fall away and turned to face the doorway. As Jayden came toward them, Felix nodded. "The team's ready?"

"A package arrived that you need to see. I'll see that Harmony is returned to her room safely."

Clearing her throat, she brought the attention back to her. "I can make it there myself."

"No. Until I return, Jayden or another guard will be with you. I won't have a repeat of last time." For the first time since they mated, there was a coldness to his voice.

"What?" Her eyes went wide, unable to believe what she was hearing.

"You heard me. I want you safe while I'm gone, and this is the only way. If Henry gets around the team and me, he'll head for you. Ty doesn't have the connection with you to insure you're safe." He stepped toward her, but when she stepped back away from him, sadness filled his gaze before he turned and left.

The tigress within her demanded she go after him, to tell him she loved him, to feel his arms around her again, but the human side of her was too angry. How dare he assign her a babysitter? Did he think he could control her as Henry once did? If so, he had another thing coming. It was time she stood up for herself.

* * *

A group gathered around a small table near the main gate to the compound, a local delivery service truck parked just beyond the gate with two guards and Raja questioning him. Felix jogged to the table, coming to stand next to Ty. "What's happening?"

"A package for Harmony was delivered by him." Ty tipped his head in the direction of the person Raja questioned. "It's already been cleared of any danger."

"I can smell the metallic taste of blood seeping into the cardboard." Felix bit out the words while trying not to breath in the horrid air.

"Human blood and fresh." Ty leaned forward, slicing through the clear packaging tape as he spoke. "Looks like Henry took it to a drop-off center forty minutes ago and paid an outrageous fee to have the delivery guy bring it out even though they were closing when he entered."

Carefully they tugged back the folds of the cardboard box, sending the stench of blood through the air. Felix's beast rose in him as the scent of blood hit him full force. There on top laid a torn piece of notebook paper, the blood already staining it red in several places.

Harmony,

You lured me to this frozen piece of land my twin calls home hours before you claimed him as a mate. Come to me within the hour at this man's home or your mate's blood will be on your hands, and then I'll hunt you down and make you pay.

Dearest twin,

I'm sure you will read this as well. You always pitied me because I couldn't shift, but my beast has given me things yours never will. Come with your mate. It's long past when we should have settled this between us.

Careful to avoid the wet blood, Felix handed the paper to Ty and looked inside the box. Pushing aside the newspaper, Felix found the cause of the blood.

"Shit!" Felix hissed. The head of the town's vet laid surrounded by the newspaper, the blood still fresh, the eyes staring but not seeing. Even though the clan never used a veterinarian, it was a small town and everyone knew who Doctor James was. When the residents found out he was murdered, it would shake the sleepy town to its core.

"Fuck!" Ty exclaimed. "You know where he lives—get the team and go. I'll deal with this. Once Henry has been neutralized, we'll send in a team to deal with his body."

Felix tore his gaze from the head and forced his attention onto Ty. "Are you suggesting we cover this up?"

"We have little choice. Someone could have seen Henry and Doctor James together. You're twins. We can't bring that pressure down on the compound now, not with all that's going on. He'll get justice for his murder, and that's what matters. No family will come looking for him. He's been a widower for over ten years, and there were no children or other family." Ty tossed the letter on the table. "Being the Alpha means protecting the clan from any harm. This scandal will harm our clan. We'll give him a proper burial, and justice will be served. That is all we can do."

Felix wanted to argue, but he couldn't. This wouldn't have been the first time the clan had covered something up nor would it be the last, but this close to home—and someone they knew—it seemed wrong on a whole different scale. Nevertheless, if they didn't and someone saw Henry with Doctor James, it would put suspicion on Felix and the clan. With the coming threats to the clan, they didn't need that, nor did they need anyone put in jail. A shifter couldn't survive there without being found out. They had to shift or their beast would eventually take over. There was no way to hide shifting into a massive tiger in a jail cell.

With no other alternative, Felix nodded. "Very well. I'll call once we've eliminated Henry."

"Watch your back. This shit with you and Henry goes back years. He's had time to let the grudge grow, and that makes him more dangerous. Don't underestimate him just because he doesn't change his form," Ty called as Felix began to walk toward the area where his team gathered.

Felix could have told him that things would be fine, but it felt like too much of a lie. Even if the mission went down without a hitch, there was still the fact he was about to kill his twin. *To protect my mate...*

Trusting a Tiger: Alaskan Tigers

Chapter Fifteen

Harmony was beyond tired of feeling like a prisoner. Every move she made was watched. Jayden led her back from the cafeteria only to stand guard outside her door. Even if there had been another exit, he'd have smelled her tigress escaping. If she wanted to have the privileges the other clan members had, then she had to make the commitment to Ty.

She collapsed on the unmade bed, feeling sorry for herself. The tiredness she was fighting earlier was nowhere to be found. Her nerves and anger over Felix hunting down Henry had cleared it away. The thought of Henry made her mentally kick herself again. She acted like such a bitch to Felix when she should have told him she loved him. If Henry killed her mate, the last words she would have said to Felix would have been in anger. How was she supposed to live with that?

For a brief moment, she thought of calling him, to apologize for her actions, but she didn't want to throw off his concentration by reminding him of how childish she had been. If he returned…no, *when* he returned, she would have to make her actions up to him.

A knock echoed within the small room. Expecting it to be Jayden, she hollered, "Come in." Sitting up, she tried to hide the irritation at being disturbed.

The door opened, revealing Tex with his white cowboy hat still firmly in place. "I'm sorry to bother you, but Doc asked me to give this to you." He held out a piece of paper toward her.

Without moving from the bed, she reached out to take the paper. "Why you? I'm sure you had more important things to do than play messenger." With the paper in her hands, she clenched it, wondering what Doc's test said. Her mixed feelings about having Daisy as a cousin turned her stomach. If Felix and the team didn't manage to dispel the threat of Henry, it would put Daisy in danger— one more person that Henry could use to control her.

"I was about to start my first shift as one of the grounds guards." He slid his hands into the pockets of his jeans, his shoulders tight with unease. "Actually, Robin was asked, but she passed. I believe she needs a little time before seeing you again. The scene over coffee has her worked up."

"I don't mean to cause any problems. Hell, that's why I left to go after Henry myself." She shook her head, her hair falling into her face. "Oh, I'm making a mess of things, aren't I?"

He remained silent until she looked up at him. "What do you want me to say?"

"Tell me I'm not screwing everything up. That would be a start." She longed to hear someone tell her that things would work out, that she wasn't throwing everything she wanted to the wind because of her fears.

"I can't do that. You already know how I feel about the situation. Have a good night, Harmony." His voice held a touch of coldness to it.

"Tex…" She called to him as he started to leave. "I appreciate you bringing this to me. No that's not it…I'm sorry. Maybe I am making a mess of this, but how do I let go of the terrors that are controlling my actions? How do I regain the control again?"

He leaned against the wall, his hand still on the door, watching her. "That's not something I can tell you—it's something you have to figure out for yourself. If you don't figure it out soon, there's going to be nothing left of what you could have had except Felix. He'll stick by you because he's your mate. The bond between you two would be too strong for anything else. But the rest of the clan, it would be an uphill battle for you to be completely one of them. Burnt bridges take twice as long to build as new ones."

With that, he left, leaving her holding the paper that now seemed to weigh more than it should. She took a deep breath and unfolded the paper until it lay open in her hands. Her heart beat against her chest with such speed that she thought it might break free. "What does it matter if we're related? She's safe here. There's no way Henry can get to her on the compound." Even as she reassured herself, her stomach twisted until she felt like she would be sick.

There's no need to go into the technical aspects of the test, only that she is your cousin.

The words on the page stole the last remaining control she had on her emotions. *A cousin.* Daisy was the only family Harmony had left. Would she be able to move past the fact that Harmony was the reason behind her imprisonment?

Falling back on the bed, she tried to take it all in, to wrap her mind around everything that had happened over the last few weeks. She went from it being her against the world to having a mate, a cousin and possibly a clan if she could just move past her reservations. The clan would become an extended family if only she'd allow them.

Throwing caution to the wind, she rose up on her elbows. "Jayden," she called, knowing he could hear her without any problems.

The door swung open, and Jayden's bulky frame stood in the doorway. "You called?" His voice held a touch of amusement, and she could guess why. She complained about him guarding her the whole time he escorted her back, and now she was calling him in. It either meant she wanted to bitch more or she needed him.

"Can you get word to Ty? I need to see him immediately."

He nodded, the smile still curving his lips. "He's busy dealing with other things, but I'll let him know that, when he's done, you've requested to see him." He turned to leave before turning back to her again. "I suspect it will take some time before Ty can tear himself away from the issue he's dealing with, so why don't you get some sleep while you wait?"

"Is that a nice way of saying I look exhausted?" She teased, and for the first time since she'd arrived, she felt lighthearted.

"I know better than to say 'yes' to that question. Rest." He shut the door before she had time to reply.

"Men—they always want you to look your best." Exhaustion tugged at her as she laid back down, tugging the blanket over her. Snuggling against the pillow, Felix's scent wrapped around her like a well-loved blanket. Everything was going to work out.

* * *

Sliding the SUV into park, Felix turned in his seat to look at the team. They were less than a half a mile from Doctor James' land. His home and office were together, sitting just far enough back the private drive that if you weren't a local you'd have continued past. How did Henry ever find the town's vet?

"Adam and I will take point. Taber and Styx, I want you to go around back. We'll hit the house at the same time. Meanwhile, Galen, I want you to stay in the SUV. When things are secure and if we need you, you can drive up." He tossed an earpiece to Galen. "Channel four, you'll hear everything that happens. If you need us, use it. Otherwise, we'll contact you when it's safe."

"Let's do this," Taber said, slipping his assault rifle over his head.

Felix nodded. "Remember, if possible, this is my kill."

After Taber and Styx slid out of the SUV, Adam turned to Felix. "Are you sure? You don't have to do this."

"I'm fine. Brother or not, he'll pay for what he did to my mate, and for what he did to others under the Ohio Alpha's command." Felix opened the door, moving slightly so that his black boots hit the ground before taking his gaze from Adam and stepping out. "Let's end this. We have other threats we need to deal with. Once we eliminate this one, we can focus on the others."

His words were callous and heartless, but inside, a little piece of him ached. Would killing his twin kill something inside of him? He suspected so, but having someone else do it would make things worse for him.

Hopping out of the SUV, Felix slung his rifle over his chest again, getting a good grip on it. The assault rifles were a new addition to the guards for missions, but they were beneficial when no one was sure what they would encounter. "Let's avoid the drive. Take the woods and stay downwind of him."

"Can he smell us?" Styx scanned the woods with determination.

"No. He doesn't have the same sense of smell we do, but I don't want us to walk into an ambush." Felix strolled toward the woods, his senses opened, scanning things as he went. Adam fell in sync with Felix's steps.

Creeping through the woods, the teams automatically separated. Felix and Adam took the direct path to the house while Taber and Styx circle around the house, keeping the points of escape in sight.

"There appears to be one door and three windows lining the back." Taber's voice crackled through the earpiece.

"Received." Felix crouched by a fallen tree, using it for cover. "Once you get as close as you can, we'll go in. Ready when you are."

Quickly surveying the land, Felix opened his shields and tried to focus enough to know where Henry was in the house. Breathing deeply, he picked up on the evergreen trees surrounding him and the wet leaves crunching under his feet before finally settling on the house. Only one person sought shelter within the walls. His tiger picked up on the body of Doctor James lying discarded in the garage where the man died.

Felix's lips curved up in a restrained growl. Henry killing then leaving the towns' veterinarian out in the garage had taken this fight to another level. "It's time. I'll end this here and now." Without turning to face Adam, Felix hit the ear bud. "Taber, guard the back entrance. Make sure he doesn't escape. Give me ten minutes with him before you come in. There's a few things that Henry and I have to discuss first."

"Take Adam." Taber voice was low and muffled, laced with the crack of branches and crunch of leaves under their boots.

"Let's go." Without waiting for an answer, Felix crept towards the front of the house. Nearing it, he drew this weapon, bringing it in front of his chest and aiming it as he went. His finger hovering just above the trigger, ready to shoot if Henry attacked as they entered. Without looking behind him, he knew Adam was doing the same. They worked together like two pieces of a whole. No orders were necessary. Felix would take right while Adam took left. It would be a fluid motion, each covering the other while searching the building.

When they found Henry, Adam would then fall back, letting Felix take the lead while still covering him.

Felix paused at the edge of the house, still in the cover of the woods. "Ready?"

"Let's do this," Adam whispered.

Without further pause, he turned around the side of the house, moving quickly up the steps. With his left hand that was steadying the assault rifle, he reached forward and twisted the doorknob. He was surprised to find it unlocked. Swinging the door open, he scanned the dark entryway, the gun moving in time with his gaze. His night vision gave him an advantage over Henry. With that knowledge, he knew Henry would be in the room ahead with the light on.

Adam must have come to the same conclusion. He nodded forward to the same room. Even knowing where he was, they eased forward, scanning each room as they went, staying alert for any traps that were waiting for them to spring.

"Brother...oh, brother, what's taking you so long? You must be looking forward to this reunion as much as I am." Henry's voice carried through the hallway on the edge of a laugh that sent a chill through Felix. It was truly an evil laugh. After years of his tiger clawing at his mind without being able to shift, Henry had finally gone truly insane.

He held up a hand, pausing Adam in his track, giving the clear message he wanted Adam to stay hidden in the hallway. Still hidden in the darkness, Felix called to his brother. "Why, Henry, why?"

"I'm not very different than you, dear twin. I fought for what I believed in."

Stepping forward, Felix left Adam in the hall. "What is that, Henry?"

Henry sat on the recliner at the far side of the room, close to the television. It had obviously been turned to face the door while Henry waited for Felix to come after him. A pistol laid in his lap, the safety was off and Henry's finger rested close to the trigger. "To destroy you. You were always the perfect one in Mom's eyes, but no longer. You'll lose this fight, and then I'll kill your mate."

"This comes down to our parent's treatment of us? We did everything we could for you, and this is how you repay us?" He didn't so much lower the rifle as point it slightly to the left of Henry.

"You call leaving me under the Ohio Alpha helping me?" Henry clenched the pistol tightly. If he had been a shifter, he'd have shattered the stock of the gun.

"I thought the clan's doctor was helping you…"

Henry shot to his feet, pulling his shirt off as he went. "Helping me! Does this look like helping?"

Angry red welts ran the length of his chest, claw marks mingled in with them, but Felix's gaze barely saw them. "What happened?"

"Don't act stupid brother…it never suited you." Henry's gaze was on him full force.

"I know nothing of what happened to you. Tell me who did it, and I'll see that they pay. We're family. I'll avenge you." A moment of regret for leaving him in Ohio made Felix wanted to lower the rifle. Then he remembered what happened to Harmony at the hands of his brother.

"You ordered it, to provoke the tiger enough to force the shift. You might not have placed the hot pokers to my skin, but you were the one behind it. It was done on your orders! It's why I went after Harmony." Henry raised the gun, pointing it at Felix seconds before squeezing the trigger.

Felix dove out of the way as the bang exploded through the room, sending the smell of gunpowder through the air. His ear bud sprang to life with Taber's voice. "Shots fired. We're coming— friendlies coming in the back door."

Adam came out of the shadows to stand just inside the door. "Don't do anything stupid, Henry. Felix never ordered what was done to you. He went to visit you countless times. You never recognized him. He would never do what you're accusing him of. If any of us would have known, we would have stopped it." While Adam had Henry's attention, it gave Felix a moment to regain his footing and get his rifle aimed on Henry again.

"Were you in on it as well? Felix never came to me, nor did my parents." Henry couldn't decide who was a bigger threat, Felix or Adam, waving the pistol between the two. "The doctor you had so much trust in kept me drugged until he could no longer keep upping the dose without risking my death. I barely knew what was happening unless they were torturing my beast to break through. Oh, they made sure I was always lucid for that."

Felix smelled more than saw Taber and Styx step into the room, their own weapons raised and ready for whatever they found. "Hold your fire," Felix ordered, his attention never leaving Henry. "How was I supposed to know when I never saw any marks on you when I visited? I thought you were getting the care I couldn't provide for you here."

"Don't stand there and try to make me hate you less! Nothing you can say will give me anything but hatred for you. You stole the life I was meant to have. I was the first born—I should have been the shifter. Instead, your accident forced the beast to come years before it should have." Henry lunged at Felix.

Without considering the options, Felix fired, shooting his twin dead center in the chest. If it was coming down to him and Henry, hands down each time he'd win. "I'm sorry, brother." Tears clouded his vision as he made his way to his fallen sibling. He kept his finger resting on the trigger until he could determine it was safe.

Stepping around the sofa, he found Henry on his back with the pistol discarded a few inches from him. Both hands covered the wound as if trying to stop the squirting blood. Felix slid the rifle to the side and reached to secure Henry's gun, knowing that Adam was right behind him with his rifle aimed at Henry's head.

"You shot me." Henry's voice crackled as blood oozed out of his mouth.

"You left me no choice." He knelt next to him, reaching out to take Henry's hand. "Why, Henry? I never wanted it to come to this." He might have never wanted it, but in his heart, he knew it would.

He knew that one day he'd have to kill Henry in order to set him free. Henry deserved better than to live inside of a body that couldn't shift, his beast driving him insane with need and pain.

Tears clouded his vision as he wrapped his arm around Henry, drawing his dying brother against his chest. "This is just the beginning for you. Soon the pain and suffering will be over." Unshed tears made his voice tight.

Memories of the years side by side, until his beast slammed a divider deep between them, flashed before his eyes. Each year his father would take them camping—a week with just the men, his father always called it. They explored the trails and caves during the days while at night they sat around the campfire making s'mores and telling ghost stories. It was a time for the three of them, one that had always haunted him as he thought back on their times together. If things had been different, it could have been Felix lying there on death's door instead.

"Randolph is gathering the rogues…" Henry coughed, spitting blood as he spoke. "Harmony knows where he is."

"I'll find him." Felix nodded. The information his twin was sharing was important, but he wanted there to be more in the final minutes of his life than more threats hanging over his head.

"Harm…she's a fighter. You've got a good mate there." Henry's fingers caught the ends of Felix's collar, dragging him closer. "I see it in your eyes that you didn't know what they did to me…I'm sorry for what I did to her."

He blinked, pushing the tears back. "As you said, she's a fighter. She'll be fine. I'll make sure of it."

"I love you, brother. I always have." His eyes fluttered, the time was running out. Felix could have called for Galen to heal Henry, but what would it have been for? There was nothing they could do for Henry, as long as he lived, he'd only suffer. They had the duty to put him down, out of his suffering.

"I love you, too." Even as the words left his lips, he knew his brother's time was up. He felt Henry's body go limp as the life left of him, the tears flowing freely down his face.

Trusting a Tiger: Alaskan Tigers

Chapter Sixteen

Harmony stood in the doorway, watching the main gate for Felix's SUV to come back. She was bubbling with the excitement she wanted to share with her mate. Seeing lights in the distance, she pushed open the door, letting the cool night air rush in past her, sending her hair flying back from her face, and stepped outside.

The headlights paused at the gate for a moment before the SUV was thrown in reverse and sped back out. Harmony rushed towards the gate, hoping the guard would know what happened. Three figures were heading towards her, each of them looking worn, their shoulders sinking as they made their way forward. Even from the distance, her night vision allowed her to see it was the team minus Felix coming toward her. What had happened? Where was her mate?

"Adam?" Tears clogged her throat, making the words garbled.

Adam jogged to her while the others peeled off, moving to the main building, except Galen who headed toward his cabin. Slinging his rifle around his back, Adam came to her and wrapped his arm around her shoulder. "Shhh, he's okay."

"Okay? Where is he? What happened?" As comforting as it was to feel another's touch, it wasn't her mate's, and that's what she wanted.

"Henry is dead, and Felix needed some time before he could face everyone. He'll be back soon."

Shaking her head, she looked up at him. "No, I have to go to him."

"Harmony, I don't know where he went. Come home with me, Robin's there and we'll have something hot to drink to shake this chill. Come on," he coaxed, but she wouldn't move from the spot she was rooted in, her gaze on the gate watching for him as if he would change his mind and come back.

She focused her mind. "Can I get a vehicle? I know where he went. I must go to him."

"Come on, I'll take you." He lead her around the building, moving quickly toward the SUVs the clan had on hand.

Now that she knew the mission was over, she had her shields open, connecting with her mate. Felix tried to block her out, but his pain was seeping into her from every corner. If it was this overwhelming for her, it had to be nearly consuming for him. "I'm on my way, love," she whispered under her breath.

"Get in. I'll grab the keys inside." Adam nodded to the first SUV before jogging to the door just to the side of the SUVs.

Climbing into the passenger side of the SUV, she wrapped her arms around her body to ward off the chill of emotions coming from her mate. He was being torn in two as a consequence of his twin's death. Felix never should have been put in the position of having to choose who to protect, his mate or his twin. Her mate was stubborn—he wouldn't have anyone else deliver the final blow to Henry. He'd rather suffer for the action than to have to look into the eyes of his brother's killer each day.

Killer? Is that how Felix sees it? She wasn't sure, but in her mind, he did the humane thing. Henry had suffered for years, now finally he was out of the misery. Either way, she vowed they'd get through it.

The driver's door flung open. Expecting Adam, she didn't turn to look. "Where are we heading?" A deeper voice asked, startling her.

She moved toward the door without thinking about it as she met the gaze of the man who opened the door. "Ty? Where's Adam?" She should have known Ty was there, her connection to the clan allowed her to sense him—to feel the draw of him—but the emotions pouring into her from Felix had her completely unaware of anything else.

"He's coming. Felix is one of my best guards, if he's in need, the clan will be there for him in every way we can. Right now you might be the best thing for him, but if he rejects the comfort you can bring, we're there as a backup. I told you before, the clan sticks together." Ty climbed in behind the wheel.

Adam pulled open the back passenger door. "All for one and one for all." With the back door closed, Ty cranked the engine and put it in reverse.

"It's amazing that the clan is that way; not all are. You're truly his family." She adjusted the comfort controls to get the heat just right.

"We're family—all of us, you included. Now let's go get your mate." Ty threw the SUV in reverse and sped out of the parking spot. "Where are we heading?"

"There's a spot above the compound that allows anyone standing there to look over it. If you go out there and turn right, follow it until...I'm not sure when, but there's a dirt road." She watched out the window, doubting herself. How was she ever going to find the place again without Felix to guide her? Could she tune into his feelings enough to know exactly where he is?

"Don't worry, I know where you mean. It's not far from here, so we'll be there in a few minutes." Ty sped around the building, heading to the gate. Someone must have alerted the gate guards since the automatic sliding gate was open.

While Ty drove, she tried to figure out what she'd say to Felix to make things better. There were no words to ease the pain of a loss, especially a loss at your own hands. All she would be able to offer was the comfort of her body, her touch and her love.

* * *

The rear door of the SUV was open, allowing Felix a place to sit, watching out over the compound. Since his beast sprung free, he had been working his way up the ranks of the clan. Each step bringing him closer to the top, the knowledge and understand that came with the position as well as the danger was something he thrived on.

Now his family had brought danger to his doorstep. Thankfully, there were no injuries to his clan family, but it didn't change the guilt coursing through him. Henry should have been dealt with years ago, but he had been soft, not willing to go against his family. Instead, he let his brother suffer under the hands of the Ohio Alpha. It didn't matter if he wasn't aware of the torture, he still felt responsible.

With Henry's death, he avenged Harmony, but that brought him little comfort. His mate was safe. There would no longer be a threat hanging over her head, but the anguish she endured under him could never be erased.

Lost in his own thoughts, he didn't hear the SUV pull up until the doors slammed shut. His gaze left the horizon to look back at the intruders. Harmony's long legs stepped out of the SUV, her red hair blowing in the wind. The sight of her sent a new wave of pain through him.

"Felix," she called, moving carefully toward him, the heels of her boots and the uneven terrain making it a slow process. Coming to stand in front of him, she reached out for him.

"Don't…" Against every instinct in his body, he took a step back just out of her grasp. He wanted to feel her arms around him, to find comfort in his mate's embrace, but he was a killer—he didn't deserve her.

"What?" Her arms dropped to her side, clearly hurt and disappointed by his reaction.

"I'm a killer...I'm covered in the blood of my own brother. How can you think of embracing me?" His voice was tight as he tried to keep a rein on his emotions.

Ty stepped up beside her. "You did what you had to do. There's no shame in that. You protected your mate and your clan."

"Where does family fall into it? He was my twin. Am I just supposed to forget him? To forget the memories we shared?"

"No one ever claimed it would be easy, but you did the right thing." Adam came to the other side of Harmony as he spoke. "Not only to protect the ones you care about but also by Henry. He didn't want to live as he was, and you knew that. You sought this option years ago, when no one would listen to you. You could have left someone else to do it, but that's not you. You're a man who will do what's right no matter what it costs you. Henry wouldn't have stopped until one of you was dead. How many innocent lives did you save from torture or death because of your actions tonight? Don't turn away those who care for you because you're hurting. Let us help you. We're family, all of us."

"Harmony, tell him," Ty whispered.

She stepped forward, not reaching out for him, but close enough that if he wanted to touch her, he could have. "Tonight I made my vow to Ty and the clan. I realized I wasn't running because I was scared, but because it meant I was willing to accept the whole situation. There was danger lurking in the shadows, and it was after me. I didn't want to bring it to the clan's door, but it was already here plus more that I didn't bring. Committing to the clan, I can help

Connor, it gives me a purpose, one I never had before. It also cements things between us and eliminates any problems my holding out caused. Felix, I love you."

"Oh, Harmony." Forgetting the blood, he reached for her, wrapping his arms around her until he could pull her tight against his chest. "I love you, too."

The feel of her snug against his body with her arms tightly around his torso made it worth his pain to have her safe. With no further threat to her from his twin, the scars that lay beneath her clothes were the only ones she'd ever have from anyone's hands—he'd see to that.

He stood there, his face buried in her head, completely wrapping his body and mind in her. The tiger within him relaxed, taking comfort from his mate the way only the beast knew how…by touch. If he hadn't already mated, he wasn't sure how he'd handle the flood of emotions coursing through him.

"We'll get through this." She ran her hands up the length of his back, her face pressed into his chest, her forehead resting against his collarbone.

"I know." With her in his arms, he had no doubt they'd overcome whatever lay before them. Minutes ticked by while they stood there embracing. Sometime in the middle of all of it, Ty and Adam had driven away, leaving them alone. "I should get you home and warm."

"Let's stay here for a while. You must have a blanket in the back of the SUV with the emergency kit." She leaned back just enough to look at him. "We need some time alone. Let me take your mind off things for a while."

Tempting as the offer was, he shook his head. "We can't. I'm still covered in blood—not just my clothes but my body, too."

"I've got that covered." She nodded forward to the red duffle bag that lay on the crest twenty feet away where Ty's SUV was parked. "Adam grabbed a few supplies for you, including a change of clothes."

"Ever-prepared Adam." He was always surprised that Adam remembered to cover all options. If the time ever came to being an Alpha of his own clan, he'd give anything to have Adam as his Lieutenant.

"Clean up, but don't worry about the new clothes. You can have them later." She winked at him, making it clear that she wanted to do more than just cuddle. "I'll lay out the blanket."

He did as she told him, a bottle of wine and two glasses laid on top of the clothes. "Why wine?" What did he have to celebrate after killing his brother? Nothing. It wasn't something to celebrate. Pushing them aside, he dug in further until he found the baby wipes, bottles of water, washrag and hand towel.

In quick time he took advantage of the supplies, cleaning his brother's blood from his hands and arms. Even in the dim light of the moon he could see that his shirt clung to his body from the blood, creating a wet, sticky suction between the fabric and his skin. Pulling it off, he found the blood had tainted his skin a pale pink. His jeans had splatters of blood, but they didn't cling to him the same way. He used the baby wipes to clean away the blood before using the bottle of water and wash rag to go over his skin, cleaning away all the remains of his brothers blood. He slipped into the boxer and jeans.

"Come on, it's getting chilly without you."

He spun around to see her laid out on the blanket in only her bra and panties, her pale skin nearly glowing in the moonlight. His gaze traveling down her body, taking her in completely, and his breath caught in his throat. Without further hesitation, he tossed the towel on the ground, grabbing the wine and glasses and making his way to her. In that instant, he realized they had something to celebrate—they had their mating, their lives and her commitment to the clan.

"What's the wine for?"

"For us. Adam added it. Would you like a glass?" He lowered himself to kneel on the blanket next to her.

"After." Rising up onto her knees, she brought their faces close. Her breath heated his cheeks, and she met his gaze with full force. "Right now I want to take the look of pain from your eyes. I can never replace him or make you forget, but for now I can help ease the pain."

"To keep you safe, I'd travel through hell and make it back to you. I love you, Harmony."

"Felix…" she caught his hand in hers, their gaze locking. "I understand if you're not in the mood for this. I just want to feel your body against mine, in whatever way you want."

Slowly he drew her hand to the front of his jeans. "Does this seem like I'm not interested?" Under their touch, his shaft was hard, straining against the constricting material. He pressed his lips to hers before she could stop him, using the motion to push her back against the blanket. His fingers unhooked her bra and tugged it off seconds before they collapsed back onto the ground.

He kissed across the line of her jaw until he found her earlobe. His teeth grazed over it, pulling it gently until she shuddered beneath him. His hands gliding down the length of her body, moving along the natural hourglass curves of her body. "All mine, mate." His voice was husky as he kissed down her body until he could bring one of her nipples into his mouth. He sucked it gently until the nipple stood at attention, not from the cold but with desire for him, then he let it slip out, grazing his teeth over it.

"You have too many clothes on. I thought I mentioned leaving them in the bag until I could show you my love for you." She tugged at his jeans, trying to unhook the belt.

"All in good time...now lay back while I get you naked." His hands teased along the wide curve of her hips until he could hook his fingers into the thin material of her panties. With one quick motion, he tugged them, the stitches coming apart without much effort, leaving her naked beneath him.

He rose off her, kicking off his boots before he could strip his jeans and boxers down his legs. His shaft sprang free from the material, freeing him from all restraints. Looking down at her, the moonlight glistening off her naked body, he still couldn't believe she was his. They had a rough start, but tonight marked the first night that the threat of Henry no longer hung over them, and for once he didn't see any lingering fears in her eyes. Even the scars that marred her body didn't tug at his guilt. It was like tonight was the first night together, without the past interfering with everything between them.

"Why are you looking at me like that?" She rose up from where she laid, covering herself with the second blanket.

"Don't." He stepped on the blanket so she couldn't pull it closer to her. "Don't cover yourself. Harmony, you're beautiful." He lowered himself until his body was hovering just above hers, his knees between her slightly spread legs.

"That look isn't just of desire, there's a hunger to it."

"A hunger for you. It's like I never truly saw you before, but now…now it's only us." He dragged his tongue in lazy circles around her nipple, kissing across the valley to the other and repeating the process. Meanwhile, he continued to watch her intently.

"Take me, Felix. I want to feel you inside of me. There will be plenty of other times for slow, but tonight I just want you, all of you." She ran her hand down his arms, teasing along the grooves of his muscles.

He slipped his hand between her legs, his fingers gliding between her lips before moving to slide inside of her. "Oh, yes, my mate, you are ready."

Coyly, she bit her lip, trying to act innocently. "For you, always."

Without further hesitation, he spread her legs farther, giving him more access to slide his shaft deep within her opening. The feel of her warm, wet core tore a growl from deep within him. He went into her about half way before pulling out and then thrusting the entire length of his manhood into her, filling her completely. She cried out her pleasure.

Their tempo increased with each stroke and her hips rose up to meet his, demanding more. Their hips slammed together, driving the force with each pump. The thrusts came deeper and faster, falling into a perfect rhythm. Their bodies rocked back and forth, and tension strained his muscles as he fought to hold back the release he longed for.

More angry red scratches appeared down the length of his chest. "Oh, Felix! Don't stop," she begged as her release found her, coursing through her as she threw back her head.

It only took a few more thrusts before his feral growl ripped through the night as his release followed. He collapsed breathlessly beside her. He tucked one arm under her, pulling her close and cradling her body tightly against his. He drew the blanket over them both to keep the night chill away from their naked, sweaty bodies.

"Harmony, you're amazing." His fingers caressed her side in lazy strokes. He buried his face in her hair, the sweet honey scent from her shampoo teasing along his senses. He let his eyes drift shut and enjoyed the peaceful feeling that coursed through him for the first time in—he couldn't remember how long.

Chapter Seventeen

Completely content, Harmony ran her fingers along the grooves of his abs, just enjoying the quietness between them. With Henry eliminated, there were other missions the clan would be focused on, bringing more danger to Felix and the people she now considered her family. So, enjoying the quiet moments alone with her mate made the whole thing worth it.

"What are you thinking about?" Felix inquired, his eyes still closed, and his fingers drawing lazy circles along her spine.

"The future. When we go back to the clan, you will continue your duties, and I'll start working with Connor. I'm wondering if things will ever be this peaceful between us again." She snuggled her head into the crook of his shoulder, her hand resting on his chest.

"We'll make time for it. With our jobs in the clan, we'll be working closely together. There's nothing to worry about, love." He kissed the top of her head.

She didn't want this time to end, but they both had things that needed to be done. They couldn't be selfish at the expense of the clan. The danger of Henry was no longer hanging over their heads, but there was always something else looming. "We should go back to the compound, shouldn't we?"

"We should, but…" He kissed her neck, drawing a moan from her, his hands sliding down her body.

"It pains me to say it, but not now. I should see what I could do to help Connor and Lukas. They've barely been sleeping, it's obvious that they need my help. I'm sure you can find something to do while I'm working." She teased, moving back from him to grab her long sleeve shirt.

He eased up behind her, wrapping his arms around her torso before she could get the shirt over her head, his fingers teasing her nipples until they were hard. Her head fell back onto his shoulder, and a moan escaped her lips. "All I want to do is please my mate."

"We've done that. Now we must focus. After some work, we can revisit how you can please me." Grabbing her clothes, she moved out of his reach.

"I thought tigresses were known for then insatiable sex drive." He sat sulking while she dressed.

"We are, but we are reasonable when there's work to be done. Plus, it's damn chilly out here in the cold." Her body shivered as she pulled up her jeans as if to confirm her point. "Snow is going to be returning soon."

"Returning? In Alaska I'm not sure if it ever truly leaves. It might give us a small break, but there are still places on the compound where there's still snow lingering on the ground." Now that she was dressed, it brought the fact he wasn't getting any more of her body, so he dressed as well.

She leaned against the SUV while Felix secured his weapons back in place. The assault rifle still lay on the corner of the blanket where he placed it, but his pistol and knives were back in their original places. "While you were gone, Doc's test results came back, Daisy and I are cousins."

"I'm not sure if I should say congratulations or apologize."

"Me either. It's weird to have family that I've never know." She crossed her arms over her chest. "How are we supposed to move past the fact that Pierce kidnapped her because of J.J.'s memory of me?"

He grabbed the unopened bottle of wine and two glasses before picking up his rifle and the blankets. "We'll save this for later when we have something to celebrate," he explained, slipping it back into the bag before answering her question. "I don't know. It might not be possible to move past it. Only time will say."

"Are you always full of such good news?"

"Naw, sometimes I'm quite dismal." He tossed everything except the rifle into the back of the SUV. "What do you want me to say? That it will all work out…that there's nothing to worry about? I can lie to you and tell you those things, but you'll taste the lie so it would be pointless. Only time will tell how things will work out between you two. Either way, you have me, and I'll make up for any cousin you could have had."

"You have a very big picture of yourself, don't you, mate?"

His face lit up with a smirk a mile wide. "For obvious reasons. Now come on. Let's get our duties out of the way because I want you naked beneath me before the sun comes up."

"Beneath you? Maybe I want to be on top this time."

"If you're tigress enough, be my guest." Without further teasing, he strolled around the side of the SUV and opened her door.

"What a gentleman?" She teased climbing in.

"Full service, mate. You wouldn't expect anything less."

No she couldn't have expected anything less from him. He was everything she wanted wrapped into one large package. One she pictured spending the rest of her life with, having a few cubs, and hopefully living a semi-peaceful life among his—no *their*—clan.

* * *

The pristine work station Connor set up for Harmony seemed out of place in the obviously lived-in room. The new laptop laid waiting for her in the center of the desk with a note. *Welcome to the team*. She was taken aback and completely in awe of it. Never before had she felt the sweet welcome of friends, or maybe it was family, as she did just now.

Connor wandered up beside her. "Don't feel like you're confined to this place. Take your laptop and work where you will. I've ordered another desktop with two monitors and a printer that you can take to Felix's cabin to use with the laptop. Everything should be here in a few days."

Not knowing what to say about the welcoming, she nodded. "Thank you."

"You're welcome. It's good to have you on board."

She rubbed her hands together. "What do you want me to do?"

"Actually, nothing at the moment. I've already set up the laptop to save time, you can do the custom stuff later, but for now, grab it. We're meeting with the Elders in fifteen minutes." Connor left, grabbing his own laptop before he headed out the door, leaving her alone to let everything sink in. "Ty's quarters."

She ran her fingers over the shiny silver machine that laid there calling to her. Never before had she had something new that she didn't have to trade away a piece of herself or work her fingers to the bone to get. There were going to be so many changes in her life in the coming weeks as she became used to living a true clan life.

"Mate," Felix called from behind her, pulling her attention from her new workstation.

She spun around to see him standing in the doorway, her hair flaring out around her in curly waves. "What are you doing here?"

"I thought I could accompany you to the Elder's meeting." He held out his arm in offering to her.

"Ahh, to be on the arm of the best looking tiger of the clan— that is an honor I cannot pass over." She scooped the laptop and notebook into her arm and strolled towards him. Her tigress paced within her, eager to push him against the table and have her way with him. *All in good time*, she promised her beast.

The short trip from where the geeks made their home to Ty's quarters was quick. She barely had time to get a good snuggle in with him before they arrived at Ty's doorstep. The sooner they got the meeting over with, the sooner they'd be able to get some sleep…or for her to have her way with him again.

Raja answered Ty's door before Felix could even raise his hand to knock. "Ty will join us shortly. There's been a call from Korbin and Jinx concerning the Ohio clan." As they entered, Raja turned back to the room. "Tad and Carran, now that everyone is here, if you could take your position at the door…"

"Come in, make yourself at home. There's coffee and cookies on the table." Tabitha called to them, setting another plate of cookies on the coffee table where everyone gathered. "Ty should be done shortly, and we can get started."

"Harmony." Robin rose from the couch coming to Harmony with her arms open. "Welcome to the clan, sister. I was thrilled when I felt you commit yourself to Ty and the clan." She wrapped her arms around Harmony, careful not to break the connection between mates.

"Thank you. It feels wonderful to be a part of a family, especially one that Felix thinks so highly of. I'm beginning to actually understand why." Easing out of Robin's embrace, she snuggled back against Felix, his touch easing her nerves. What also helped was the fact that Connor was sitting on the opposite side of the room, and he was counting on her.

Felix led her to the bar area where Connor had already set up. "This will be the best place for you to work. I'll be nearby." He pressed a quick kiss to lips.

She wanted to lean into him, forcing a deeper kiss between them, but in that instant, Ty came out of his office and the room quieted.

"If we could all take a seat, I have some news from Korbin and Jinx concerning the Ohio Tigers." He crossed the room in three quick strides, coming to stand beside his mate and taking her hand in his. Once everyone settled down, Ty continued. "Korbin seems to have things under control for the most part. He's asked if Adam would bring Robin down to help with some of the clan members who have suffered under the former Alpha the most."

"I told you before I'd go. Just let me know when, and Adam and I will be there." Robin ran her hand over Adam's knee, soothing the fact she just agreed for him.

Adam placed his hand over hers, interlocking their fingers. "Maybe Taber or Thorben could be spared to fly us? It would take less time than if I take the helicopter."

Ty nodded. "We can make those arrangements later, but that's a good idea since Jinx will be returning then as well. Since Korbin is being accepted, there's no reason for Jinx to stay on. However, a few of the West Virginia Tigers are staying as guards for Korbin, and if things change, Jinx could be there within a few hours. In the meantime, we need him here to make our foundation solid with Tabitha coming out, and within the coming weeks, we will have to send a team to deal with Avery. He is not meeting our demands, and his tactics are still over the top. We cannot allow what he did to Tex to continue happening to the other clan members."

Raja nodded in agreement. "Avery is threatening to send a team to collect Tex from us next week, so that might force our hand sooner."

"But that's not why we're gathered here tonight. We're here to discuss Randolph. Harmony, we believe you might know where to find him?" Ty's gaze moved over to where Harmony sat taking notes on her laptop.

"I what? I don't believe I even know a Randolph."

"Randolph is a lone tiger. He's been preaching the need to kill Tabitha before she can bring all the tigers together. He's gathering the rogues as we speak to continue where Pierce left off. When Henry...died, he said you would know where he was. He visited with Henry often, so you might have seen him when you were in Ohio. Adam?" Ty nodded to Adam who turned his laptop to Harmony, the picture of Randolph on screen.

"I know him..." Her hand flew to cover her mouth, her breath caught in her throat. She took a moment to gather herself. "Henry, never called him by his name, but I saw him there while Henry held me captive." She shot a quick glance to Felix to see how he was handling them talking about his brother. She felt his pain, but his face held no traces of it. He seemed relaxed, interested, but not emotionally involved. Her Felix had a hard outer shell that kept his feelings hidden, at least from everyone except her.

Memories of the times Randolph visited with Henry played through her. Those times were some of the only relaxed evenings she ever spent under Henry's control. Randolph brought homemade liquor, and the men sat in Henry's small study drinking until the hour grew late. Harmony was never included once the liquor was brought out, only expected to fetch whatever they required, yet it was a reprieve from the abuse Henry forced on her each night.

Felix eased off the wall, coming toward her. "What happened on those visits? Do you remember what they talked about?"

"I wasn't included once they brought out the hard liquor, only expected to bring them ice, food, or whatever they needed. In the winter I was also expected to tend the fire, nothing more. I don't think I can be of any help finding him. Why would I know where he is?" The laptop before her beeped, she ran her fingers over the mouse pad to wake it.

"I've sent you a map that I've been able to pinpoint Henry's location at in the last few months. See if anything looks familiar. That may be where Randolph is hiding." Connor explained the beep of the computer not only to her but to everyone else.

Felix's hand caressed her shoulder as she looked over the map. It took her moment to realize what she was looking at. There in the center of all the red dots was the main compound of the Ohio Tigers. Other dots surrounded the area where… "Oh my, that's my house. Before I was given to Henry, I had a little place just off the compound grounds, giving me privacy and keeping me out of the mix of the clan politics."

"Which one?" Felix asked, leaning over her shoulder.

"This one." She pointed to the red dot just outside of the main cluster, giving Felix a chance to look at it before pointing it out to Connor.

"Interesting…" There was a flash of something in Connor's eyes.

"What is?" Ty asked, coming closer to look at the laptop screen.

Typing away at the keyboard, Connor didn't bother to look up as he answered Ty. "The spot she's pointing at is where Henry was once he left the compound. He was there for days before starting his journey to Harmony. Did Henry know that it was your place?"

"Yes. When I was given to him, all my possessions became his as well. He'd take me there sometimes…" A shudder coursed through her body, cutting off her words.

"With his death, the property is yours again." She looked up to see that Raja had joined them sometime during the mix of it all.

"I don't want it. Burn it, sell it—honestly, I don't care. It holds too many bad memories for me to see it again. Even if it didn't, this is my home now." She placed her hand over Felix's that was still on her shoulder.

"Very well. I'll have Korbin see to it, and the proceeds for selling the house will be sent to you." Raja nodded to the computer. "Do you think Randolph might be there? Would there be enough room for the rogues to gather."

"Not in the house, no, but the security is top of the line. He'd know if someone was coming from a quarter of a mile away. Wait…" She closed her eyes, trying to get the memory back in full. With her eyes closed, she could see the clearing in the woods and almost smell the lush trees and damp grass. The clan had once gathered, but when they had to sell off part of the land, she now knew the Alpha used the money to help Pierce. "I know where they are."

Her eyelids sprang open, and she found everyone staring at her, waiting for her to explain. "A few years ago, the Alpha sold off land that had once been part of the compound in Ohio. It allowed me to buy the house and the land surrounding it. There's a large clearing a good distance in the wood, it's where the clan would gather for celebrations and clan business."

"I don't understand how any of this has anything to do with Randolph, he was never a part of the clan." Ty accepted the coffee Tabitha offered.

"Under the celebration grounds there are living quarters. It's where the Elders would meet for private meetings. Randolph knows the area, he attended some of the clan's celebrations. If I'm supposed to know where they are, it has to be the celebration grounds." She tugged a hand through her hair, trying to get rid of the unease of everyone watching her. "Instead of selling the house and land, I think it should go back to the clan. Raja if you could make arrangements for Korbin to regain control of the home and land for the clan I'd appreciate it."

"I'll see to it." Raja nodded.

"Raja and I will get in touch with Korbin after the meeting and have a team check the grounds to see if Randolph or any of the rogues are there. For now I believe that's all we have. Connor, I want you three seeing if you can find out anything else on any of the rogues on the list you have. There's three of you now, divide and conquer the list. Also, continue to monitor the situation in Texas. Felix, make sure Harmony is brought up to speed on all clan business. It looks like Tabitha will be announcing herself as the Queen of Tigers soon. The magical book that has helped her through everything so far has told her that she would have to make the announcement before we take on the Texas Tigers for the other clans to fall in line." With the mention of his mate, Ty slid his arm around Tabitha.

"What happens if the clans don't fall in line?" Harmony wasn't sure she understood everything, but she had to ask.

"We are aware there's going to be rebellion as I claim my place as the Queen of the Tigers, which is why we have the guards. Felix, Adam, Thomas, Shadow, Styx, and everyone else are excellent at what they do, I have no doubt they will keep everyone safe. The Kodiak Bears, West Virginia Tigers, and now Carran are wonderful additions that make us stronger. If anyone chooses to take us on, they will have a strong fight on their hands. We will come out on top in the end, and everything we went through to get there will be worth it."

With Tabitha's words, Harmony couldn't help but wonder if it would be worth the cost at the end. Would they lose too many of those they cared for before they reached the end? Her poor Felix had already been forced to kill his twin to keep her and the clan safe. For some, that would have already been too much of a cost.

Chapter Eighteen

The sun was already sinking low into the sky, and dusk was beginning to fall upon the compound when Felix finally woke. Harmony's body pressed tightly against his side, her arm draped over him, holding him securely. Teasing his finger along her shoulder, he woke her gently. "Love."

"Ummm." She snuggled in closer to him and deeper under the covers. "Too early."

"It's nearly dinner time." He tucked her hair behind her ear.

"It also means I have another two hours until we're supposed to report. Tabitha isn't expecting you yet…can't you just go back to sleep?"

"Work isn't what's on my mind. I was thinking there's another way we can spend the next two hours." His hand travel down her body, his mouth finding hers just before his cell phone rang, stealing the moment away.

"Duty calls," she whispered, her voice fully awake.

"Forget it…" The tug of his duty to his clan weighed on him and made his voice tight.

"No, you know you can't do that. Answer it. I know you'll make up for it later."

Knowing she was right, he rolled over and snatched his cell from the nightstand. Sliding his finger over the screen to answer, he brought it to his ear and growled. "Hello."

"Robin's just returned from her session with Daisy. Things are going better than expected there." Felix could here Ty sitting behind his desk, shuffling papers.

"You didn't call to give me the update on Robin's session, so with all due respect, could we get to the point? I was about to use my last two-hour break for some recreational activities."

Ty sighed. It was almost as if the Alpha was trying to work up to it, which was completely against Ty's nature. "Daisy has asked that Harmony visit her. She'd like to see the only family she has left."

"Absolutely not!"

"I had a feeling you'd say that, but, Felix, if Daisy commits to the clan, the women will see each other. They are the only true blood family either of them have." Ty leaned back, the chair squeaking as he did. "I'm not asking you to let her go alone. Hell, I don't even allow Robin to do her sessions without Adam or another guard to protect her."

Felix tried not to let his anger taint the words to his Alpha, but it wasn't working as he expected. "I don't care if there's a dozen guards armed to the teeth, she's not going. Daisy is unpredictable right now, especially with what she's been through and why she was chosen. You wouldn't allow Tabitha to go either, so don't ask me to do this."

"I'm only asking that you speak with your mate on the subject. Keeping her from Daisy could cause backlash for you. When all is said and done, it's your decision. Either way, I'll expect to see you both at work in two hours. Call if you need more guards to go with you." Ty laughed and clicked off.

Was his Alpha trying to hint that Felix would take Harmony to visit her cousin? If so it wasn't working. He'd stand firm to keep his mate safe. Laying the phone aside, he had every intention of picking up where he left off.

"What about Daisy? Is she okay?" Harmony was no longer snuggled next to him. She lay a few inches away, propped up on her elbow glaring at him.

"She's fine. Now where were we?" He leaned into her only to be pushed back.

"You're not telling me something." She raised an eyebrow at him, waiting.

"I take it I won't be enjoying your beautiful body before we get to work?" he asked only to have her continue to stare at him. "It's a crying shame." Rolling onto his back, he closed his eyes, hoping her tigress couldn't resist another romp in the hay before a night of work.

"What the hell are you doing?" Rising to sit, she tugged the sheet with her to keep her body covered.

He refused to open his eyes, not giving in to her demand for information on Daisy, she'd find out soon enough, and then he'd have a fight on his hand with his high-spirited mate. "If I can't make love to my beautiful mate, I might as well use this time to sleep."

"There's no way in hell you're going to sleep until you tell me what's happening with Daisy. As her cousin, don't I have a right to know if there's something wrong with her?"

"Goodnight, my mate."

A growl echoed through the small room that they took over in the main compound building. "Felix, do I look like I'm playing? You're not going to get any sleep or sex until you tell me what's going on. I'll go find out for myself if I have to."

Harmony waited while he continued to pretend to sleep until she had enough and moved to let her legs fall over the edge of the bed. The beast within refused to let her go away angry. "I'm sorry."

Pausing at the edge of the bed, she turned back to look at him. "If that's the truth, then tell me what's happening with Daisy."

"She wants to see you." He barely got the words out when she pushed off the bed, the sheet going with her in one clean movement.

"What?"

"I'm not sure how much clearer I can make it. Your cousin wants to see you." Forgetting sleep, he sat up in the bed. "It's not happening so come back to bed."

"What?"

Smirking, he couldn't help but tease her. "My dear Harmony, what happened to your vocabulary that you're now limited to only one word?"

"What I don't understand is why you're telling me what I am and am not going to do." She snatched her robe off the edge of the bed and wrapped it around her body, tossing the sheet back onto the bed.

He suppressed a snarl as she covered up her beautiful body. "We don't know what she is capable of yet, and I won't risk you. She needs time to adjust, to work through her issues. Seeing you now could only serve as a reminder of why she was taken by Pierce in the first place. I won't risk you."

"Risk me? What the hell do you think this is? Just because we're mated doesn't give you the right to decide what's right for me."

So this is what Ty was hinting at? Harmony would wear him down to take her to see Daisy. How did mates deal with this? "Harmony, I'm only protecting you."

"I don't need protection." Collapsing on the bed as if the air went out of her, the spark of fight that was in her eyes had gone.

"What is it, mate?" He leaned forward, clasping her hand. The comforter fell past his hips, revealing his naked body.

A sigh escaped between her lips, her shoulders sinking. "I hate to admit it, but maybe your right. No matter, we're family, and I should see her."

"Well, if I'm not getting sex and can't sleep, then I'm going to shower. We can discuss this once we're dressed." He threw off the blanket and stepped out of the bed. Anything to put off fighting with his mate when he wasn't allowing her to go to Daisy's.

* * *

Harmony smoothed her hair, trying to repair the damage the wind did. She wanted to make a good impression on Daisy, not look like a wind-blown mess, it was bad enough she only had twenty minutes before she and Felix had to report to duty.

"I would like to make my objections known that this is a bad idea. You could do more harm to her, walking through this door. Is that what you really want?" Felix stood beside her, his hand on the gun nestled in the shoulder holster.

"I have to agree. Daisy is in a very delicate state right now." Styx stood just behind them. He was armed as well, but his hand wasn't touching his gun, not that it made him any less intimidating. There was something about him that screamed danger.

"Yet, if I refuse her request, it could erect the wall to divide me from the only blood family I have left. Now we're going in, if you two want to wait here, be my guest. Scared of a little tigress." She turned the handle, letting herself in.

"In your dream, mate," Felix whispered before pushing his way in front of her. "Remember, you're mated. Women are protected."

The Alaskan Tigers concept that the mated females and children should be protected was a new concept to her. In Ohio it didn't matter your sex—if you were of fighting age, you fought for the clan. Not that she had to do much of that. Having her house off the compound had kept her from most of the clan's politics. It was that final fight that proved she was weak and was the invitation for her former Alpha to give her to Henry. She shook her head, refusing to think about the past. After all, things had come full circle for her, and she had found her mate and an extended family within the clan.

Looking around the small cabin, she was surprised that it was bigger than the room her and Felix currently shared in the main building. Ty had put Daisy in one of the clan guest cabins on the far side of the compound, offering her a chance to adjust to her newfound freedom. It was completely open, a one-room cabin, but it still didn't feel cramped. The small kitchenette was just to the right of the doorway, with the living area and bedroom space taking up the back portion.

Daisy sat in the middle of the bed, the blankets twisted up, making a nest around her, and a bound journal lay open in her lap. She had long red hair just a shade or two lighter than Harmony's. Her thin frame was covered with a bulky turtleneck sweater and jeans. The sweater struck Harmony as odd. Even with the cool Alaska weather at this time, it was still too warm for a turtleneck.

Styx closed the door behind them, and suddenly she felt trapped. This was a bad idea and too late to turn around. Taking a deep breath, she stepped around Felix. "Daisy, you asked to see me?"

Daisy sat her journal aside, watching them intently. "We do look alike, don't we? No wonder Pierce made the mistake."

"Time is limited, Daisy. What is it you wanted to see her about?" Felix inquired, his hand still resting on his weapon.

"I wanted to see the woman that caused the months of torture I suffered." Daisy shot off the bed with such speed, Harmony fought not to take a step back. "After your Alpha rescued me, you'd still shoot me?"

Until Daisy spoke, Harmony didn't even realize that Felix and Styx both drew their weapons. She didn't tell the men to put their weapons up, because the way this was going, they might have no choice but to use them. Instead she focused on her cousin. "You wanted to see me to make me feel guilty? If that's your motive, you're too late, but I'm not directly responsible for what happened to you, nor did I know anything about it until we both ended up here. I'm sorry for what happened to you."

"You're sorry!" Daisy screamed, dashing around the bed, heading straight for them. "That doesn't change a bloody thing! It doesn't take away the scars on my body, the brand he burned into my right hip."

"If you come any closer, you will leave me no choice." Felix stepped forward, cutting off Daisy's access to Harmony.

"There's nothing more to say then. I'm sorry, but you're not the only one that suffered. I'm not making light of what happened to you, but you have your whole life ahead of you. Let Robin help you so that you can have a life now that you're free." She knew it was harsh, but Daisy needed someone to say it. Everyone was moving around her as if she was going to break down any moment. She couldn't continue to live hidden in this small cabin indefinitely. If she had to say the harsh words to get Daisy to pull herself up by her bootstraps and put the pieces back together, then so be it.

Daisy lunged at her, and in that instant, Styx pushed her aside and fired. "No!" Harmony cried as she stumbled out of the way, but it was too late. The trigger was pulled, and the bullet had exited the chamber.

Felix wrapped his arm around her, his gun still in hand. "It's okay, it's only a tranquilizer gun. She'll be knocked out for a few hours and one mighty pissed off tigress when she wakes, but you're safe."

Daisy crumpled onto the floor in a heap, her eyes glazed over as the drugs hit her system. The look on her face was pure hatred. Harmony couldn't believe the hatred that was coming over Daisy in waves. They'd never be able to move past something that beyond their control. It had been the cement of the relationship that could never be.

"You okay? I need to help Styx get her onto the bed." Felix stood in front of her watching her, his hands on either shoulder.

She took a moment to realize that they had moved while she was lost in her thoughts. "Go, I'm fine." He lingered for a moment, not sure if he believed her before stepping away to help Styx but leaving her to grieve the last piece of her family.

Today Styx had shown her why Felix trusted him to keep her safe. He was a warrior with heart and character beyond many others. Felix didn't work together as smoothly with Styx as he did with Adam, but there was still a strong connection between the guards— one that went back many years.

The two men lifted Daisy onto the bed before coming across the room to her again. Felix wrapped his arm around her, securing her tightly against his body. "I'll get another guard for the door, one is no longer enough."

Styx nodded. "I'll wait here until one has been assigned."

"Very well. Then you're off for the evening unless something happens. Come on, mate." Felix steered her towards the door with Styx following a few steps behind her.

Stopping a few inches from the door, she spun around to face him. "Thank you, Styx. I owe you more than words for saving my life."

"You own me nothing. You are one of us, and we protect our own." He gave her a smile, his hand reaching hers to squeeze it slightly.

Even though she could feel the honesty of his words, she still felt indebted to him. For now she let it go, maybe one day she'd find a way to repay him. Or take away the pain she saw in his eyes.

Chapter Nineteen

Felix leaned against the counter watching Tabitha, Bethany, Robin and Harmony cook dinner. Everything was once again calm. Even Daisy had caused no more problems since Harmony's visit. He was dealing with his grief and the loss of his twin. Harmony was adjusting well to the clan and had quickly made friends with the Elder mates.

Watching them work with such ease, he was impressed with how well Harmony fit in, creating a dinner for their mates while Shadow, Adam and Felix stood observing. Shadow was the only unmated shifter attending the small friendly dinner, but it didn't seem to bother her. She was on duty anyways, so enjoying a dinner with her charge was not out of the ordinary.

Shadow propped up on the bar stood and tugged her laptop from the bag sitting on the counter. She looked more like a college student with her tight boot-cut blue jeans and grey and white sweater that hung off her shoulders. Her fingers flew over the keyboard, doing heaven only knows what. All the time working side jobs for Connor in the downtime from guarding Bethany had greatly increased her computer knowledge.

"Shadow, what does Connor have you looking into now?" Felix lowered himself to her as well.

"Actually, I'm looking over the blueprints of Manetka Resort. The hotel owned by Avery. Catering to the shifters had some secrets of its own. There's a number of secret passages linking it to other buildings. If we could corner Avery outside of the resort, it might be our best plan." She turned the screen enough for Felix and Adam to see it.

"Why did he ask you?" Felix couldn't keep the surprise out of his voice. Shadow was an amazing guard—one of the best—that she was the only female guard in the clan was high praise to her skills. It was also why she was the Captain of the Guards for the Lieutenant's mate, Bethany.

"Don't act so surprised. I speak Polish, and there's a lot of Polish words on the map and documents. For Connor to translate it, it would take time that we don't have, especially with Avery becoming more and more demanding. I offered to look at it and see what I can decipher."

Robin slid the casserole dish back into the oven before looking over her shoulder to Adam. "Manetka? I remember you were going to take me there when we were in Texas."

"Yes. Manetka—the Polish word for shifter—was supposed to be safe haven for their kind. Hopefully once we eliminate Avery, it can once again be that place." Adam explained.

Felix nodded, there were going to be major changes in Texas, and it would once again be a safe place for shifters. "It will be. We need safe places like that around the country. Korbin is thinking about using part of the grounds just to the south of the Ohio compound that he inherited as a similar resort. There's an old warehouse there that, with some work, could be a safe place for shifters as well as provide more space for his clan."

"That reminds me—I promised Tex I'd check on him after his shift. With my part of dinner in the oven, mind if I slip off for a bit?" Harmony asked.

"Go ahead. Take Felix with you. We'll be fine." Tabitha sliced the vegetables, adding them to the pan before her.

"Come, my mate." Felix held his hand out to her. They had nearly an hour and half before they had to be back for dinner. Maybe a few quiet minutes after their visit with Tex wouldn't be out of the question. He'd never get enough of his mate's body.

The clan still had a number of uphill battles before them, putting them all at danger. Every indication Tabitha's magical book gave them said her reveal, being the Queen of the Tigers was nearing. Now it was just a waiting game for them all. The threat of Avery and rogues were looming as well, waiting for them to deal with.

Leading Harmony from Tabitha's quarters, he vowed to make a few minutes with his mate after the visit with Tex. After all, he had to enjoy the quiet time before things got dangerous again.

Trusting a Tiger: Alaskan Tigers

Marissa Dobson

Born and raised in the Pittsburgh, Pennsylvania area, Marissa Dobson now resides about an hour from Washington, D.C. She's a lady who likes to keep busy, and is always busy doing something. With two different college degrees, she believes you're never done learning.

Being the first daughter to an avid reader, this gave her the advantage of learning to read at a young age. Since learning to read she has always had her nose in a book. It wasn't until she was a teenager that she started writing down the stories she came up with.

Marissa is blessed with a wonderful supportive husband, Thomas. He's her other half and allows her to stay home and pursue her writing. He puts up with all her quirks and listens to her brainstorm in the middle of the night.

Her writing buddies Max (a cocker spaniel) and Dawne (a beagle mix) are always around to listen to her bounce ideas off them. They might not be able to answer, but they are helpful in their own ways.

She love to hear from readers so send her an email at marissa@marissadobson.com or visit her online at http://www.marissadobson.com.

Trusting a Tiger: Alaskan Tigers

Other Books by Marissa Dobson

Tiger Time

The Tiger's Heart

Tigress for Two

Night with a Tiger

Trusting a Tiger

Snowy Fate

Sarah's Fate

Mason's Fate

As Fate Would Have It

Learning to Live

Learning What Love Is

Her Cowboy's Heart

Half Moon Harbor Resort Volume One

Passing On

Reaping Good Time

Restoring Love

Winterbloom

Unexpected Forever

Losing to Win

Praise

Alaskan Tigers

Tiger Time:

This is the first book that I have read from Marissa Dobson and it definitely won't be my last. I loved the tiger shapeshifter aspect of this book which I haven't read much about in previous books. ~ Jennifer at Books-n-Kisses

When I first read a review for Tiger Time, I knew this was a must read. Now I know that it is definitely a must read for anyone that like were romances. It's definitely one of those that draws you immediately into the story, and never lets you go… a wonderfully written story of a woman's journey into the unknown and a man who would show her to her destiny. LOVED IT!!!! Looking forward to the next one in the series. ~ Addicted to Romance

The Tiger's Heart:

This book was so interesting and I loved it. Steamy with lots of twists and turns. Recommend this to anyone who likes Shifter type books. ~ Amazon Reader

Tigress for Two:

And the plot thickens. I am really enjoying how the overall story arc of this series is going. There are so many players that it is fascinating to watch the plot unfold. Everyone's story is connected, but not in the ways that I had originally anticipated and that makes it all the more fun to read. ~ Delphina Reads too Much

Wow, Tigress for Two was everything I'd hoped it would be after reading some of Marissa Dobson's other books. She packed a whollop, enticing the reader with angst, suspense, romance and suspense…oh did I say that twice? Well good cause I meant to, because she did a great job of keeping the reader in suspense throughout the whole story. I never knew what was coming next but i was so intrigued I couldn't put the book down. I seriously never imagined mixing shifter species but it was done well. ~ A Passion for Romance

Stormkin Series

Storm Queen:

To use the word amazing is not too strong when describing this book. I've never read anything like it and I loved every minute of it. Do yourself a favor of buying this book, if you don't you'll be missing out. ~Rebecca Royce, bestselling author of the The Westervelt Wolves.

This was a great new addition to the paranormal romance world, it almost had a Urban Fantasy feel because the sex wasn't the main focus of the story and I LOVED that! I thought each scene was done so well! I will be continuing this series! I can't wait for the next one! ~ Amazon Reader

Clearwater Series

Winterblom:

I found Winterbloom to be a sweet and delightful little romance. Ms. Dobson does a wonderful job of creating visual scenes that allow the reader to feel as though they are right there within the story. ~ Romancing the Book

Unexpected Forever:

Unexpected Forever made me cry. I'll admit it; I teared up quite a few times actually…Marissa has yet again written an amazing story full of emotions and detail. I totally recommend reading Unexpected Forever and other great works by Marissa. ~ Crystal Out There

Fate Series

As Fate Would Have It:

This book has all 3 of the Fate Stories in it! Each are about mountain lion shifters and finding their mates! All are sweet, Heartwarming, Romantic stories! I can't wait to read more by Marissa Dobson! ~Amazon Reader

Snowy Fate:

This was a very quick read, but with just a few pages, Marissa Dobson is able to get to the heart of this story. ~ Cocktails & Books

I really enjoyed Snowy Fate. I hope that you take the time to learn that no matter how hard you try you can't fight fate. ~ Books-n-Kisses

I thought this one was just perfect in length. There was enough background that I felt I knew the characters well and their attraction was believable. Fate has a way of making a HEA very real. I definitely recommend this one! ~ From the TBR Pile

CPSIA information can be obtained at www.ICGtesting.com
Printed in the USA
LVOW13s2307250614

391664LV00001B/262/P